THE HELLBOUND HEART

Clive Barker was born in Liverpool in 1952. In addition to his work as a novelist, short-story writer and illustrator, he also writes, directs and produces for the stage and screen. In 1987 he made his debut as a film director and writer of the highly successful *Hellraiser*, based on his story *The Hellbound Heart*. He is the author of *The Books of Blood*, *The Damnation Game*, *Weaveworld*, *Cabal*, and *The Great and Secret Show*. His latest book is *Imajica*. Clive Barker lives in Los Angeles.

CLIVE BARKER

'A powerful and fascinating writer with a brilliant imagination . . . an outstanding storyteller.'

J. G. BALLARD

'Mr Barker certainly extends one's appreciation of the possible. He is a fine writer.' *Wall Street Journal*

'Clive Barker has been an amazing writer from his first appearance, with the great gifts of invention and commitment to his own vision stamped on every page.'

PETER STRAUB

'Barker is so good I am almost tongue-tied. What Barker does makes the rest of us look like we've been asleep for the last ten years. His stories are compulsorily readable and original. He is an important, exciting and enormously saleable writer.' STEPHEN KING

'Mixing elements of horror fiction and surrealist literature, Barker's work reads like a cross between Stephen King and Gabriel Garcia Marquez. He creates a world where our biggest fears appear to be our own dreams.'
Boston Herald

'Prodigiously talented . . . Barker can write weirdness like no one else.' *City Limits*

'Barker's visions are at one turn horrifying and at the next flickering with brilliant invention that leaves the reader shaking, not with fear, but with wonder.'
Sounds

CLIVE BARKER's Films

HELLRAISER

'Barker's dazzling debut creates such an atmosphere of dread that the astonishing set-pieces simply detonate in a chain reaction of cumulative intensity . . . a serious, intelligent and disturbing horror film. *Hellraiser* will leave you, to coin one of Barker's own phrases, in a state between hysteria and ecstasy.'   *Time Out*

'The best horror film ever to be made in Britain.'
Melody Maker

'A real marrow-melter . . . it plays on the darkest fears and fantastical obsessions of the human psyche . . . chilling and compelling.'   *The Scotsman*

'Want to see something *really* scary? Barker exploits our deepest dreads about pain equals pleasure and the fears that our socially repressed primal desires will one day unloose and end in a sexual nightmare.'
City Limits

'Bizarre and gruesome . . . one of the few movies that comes out of the screen at you. Imaginative, classy, unique, compelling and robust.'   *Venue*

'The best slam-bang, no-holds-barred, scare-the-shit-out-of-you horror movie for quite a while.'
Screen International

'Gore galore and biting wit make Barker's gothic chiller a real scream.'   *Time Out*

'A nightmarish tale about creatures from a realm of ultimate pain and torture. Startlingly gruesome.'

Toronto Star

'Evocatively creepy.'

New York Times

'Barker has achieved a fine degree of menace.'

Daily Telegraph

'A pinnacle of the genre.'

Daily Mail

'The best horror movie of the year.'

New Musical Express

'Raising the scares that other films cannot reach, *Hellraiser* is a masterpiece of cinematic horror.'

Tracks

NIGHTBREED

'A carnival feel, a breathless ghost train ride through a fantastical world of grotesquely glamorous monsters . . . it certainly has its finger on the pleasure button.'

Time Out

'Expansive and imaginative.'

The List

'Decorated with wild visual imagination and twists of plot . . . bizarre, outrageous, elaborate detail on an epic scale . . . flamboyant, inventive – it goes like a train and is notably stylish.'

Daily Mail

CLIVE BARKER's Novels

CABAL

'A complete but open-ended system of multi-layered, dark magic. On the one hand it's a simple macabre tale; on the other it shows a deep and dreadful understanding of society and its outcasts . . . a rare, powerful fantasy.'
Fear

'A gripping story of powerful erotic intensity.'
Sunday Independent

'Barker's characteristic juxtaposition of fascination and fear find eloquent expression in this novella which treats death as metamorphosis into another state of being.'
Time Out

'Barker at his terrifying best.'   *Yorkshire Evening Post*

'Confirms his status as probably the most exciting contemporary writer of fantasy/horror. Definitely a book to have you looking over your shoulder.'
Dublin Evening Herald

WEAVEWORLD

'All that you expect from Clive Barker and more — terrifying, shocking, audaciously imaginative, moving and ruthlessly unputdownable.'   RAMSEY CAMPBELL

'Prodigious imagination . . . *Weaveworld* is beguiling for its imaginative power.'
Today

'His new dark fantasy, an epic tale of a magic carpet and the wondrous world within its weave, towers above his earlier work ... it manages, via its powerful and giddy torrent of invention, to grasp the golden ring as the most ambitious and visionary horror novel of the decade ... a raging flood of image and situation so rich as to overflow. Barker has unleashed literary genius.'

Kirkus

'*Weaveworld* is pure dazzle, pure storytelling. The mixed tricky country where fantasy and horror overlap has been visited before – though not very often – and *Weaveworld* will be a guide for everyone who travels there in the future. I think it'll probably be imitated for the next decade or so, as lesser talents try to crack its code and tame its insights.'   PETER STRAUB

'His most ambitious and imaginative work ... strands of Joyce, Poe, Tolkien ... an irresistible yarn.'   *Time*

'*Weaveworld* confirms Clive Barker as a formidable talent in British dark fantasy.'   Q

'Recommended ... a fantastic tale of imagination.'

JONATHAN ROSS, *Sunday Express*

THE GREAT AND SECRET SHOW

'There is such intensity and scope to this work that I can find no flaw in this utterly perfect novel. *The Great and Secret Show* is a horror story, it is mythology, and it is a story about people, real people ... one of the most original and important works of horror fiction in a long, long time.'   *Rave Reviews*

'Rich and absorbing . . . the images are vivid, the asides incisive and the prose elegant in this joyride of a story.'
Time

'Clive Barker's career has been building up to *The Great and Secret Show*. With each book, he's been moving toward a sort of fiction that is grander than the usual horror novel but that is also a paradigm of horror fiction. If you thought Thomas Pynchon's *Vineland* was disappointingly tidy and coherent, by all means latch on to *The Great and Secret Show*. In its vast, loopy sprawl, it is nothing so much as a cross between *Gravity's Rainbow* and *Lord of the Rings*; allusive and mythic, complex and entertaining . . . extravagantly metaphorical, wildly symbolic, skillful and funny.'
New York Times Book Review

'A massive and brilliant Platonic dark fantasy that details an eruption of wonders and terrors – as the veil between the world of the senses and the world of the imagination is rent in a small California town. The torrent of invention is astounding, the total impact is staggering, as Barker creates one of the most powerful overtly metaphysical novels of recent years.'   *Kirkus*

'The best thing he has ever written . . . pure narrative simplicity . . . gore fans will get their chills, subtle horror readers will have theirs and the lighter fantasy readers will be entranced . . . what wonders are in store as he develops his themes?'   *Fear*

'Barker's imagination is mind-numbing, his invention breathtaking, his prose as polished and exquisite as ever. This is fantasy of the highest order. Quite brilliant.'
Melody Maker

CLIVE BARKER

THE HELLBOUND HEART

Fontana

An Imprint of HarperCollins*Publishers*

The Hellbound Heart was first published in Great Britain in 1987, as part of the anthology *Night Visions 3*, by Century Hutchinson.

This edition first published in 1991 by Fontana,
an imprint of HarperCollins*Publishers*,
77–85 Fulham Palace Road,
Hammersmith, London W6 8JB

9 8 7 6 5 4 3 2 1

The Author asserts the moral right to be
identified as the author of this work

A catalogue record for this book is
available from the British Library

ISBN 0 00 647065 3

Phototypeset in Sabon by Intype, London
Printed in Great Britain by
HarperCollinsManufacturing Glasgow

For Mary

'I long to talk with some old lover's ghost
Who died before the god of Love was born.'
JOHN DONNE, 'Love's Deitie'

THE HELLBOUND HEART

ONE

So intent was Frank upon solving the puzzle of Lemarchand's box that he didn't hear the great bell begin to ring. The device had been constructed by a master craftsman, and the riddle was this – that though he'd been told the box contained wonders, there simply seemed to be no way into it; no clue on any of its six black lacquered faces as to the whereabouts of the pressure points that would disengage one piece of this three-dimensional jigsaw from another.

Frank had seen similar puzzles – mostly in Hong Kong, products of the Chinese taste for making metaphysics of hard wood – but to the acuity and technical genius of the Chinese the Frenchman had brought a perverse logic that was entirely his own. If there was a system to the puzzle, Frank had failed to find it. Only after several hours of trial and error did a chance juxtaposition of thumbs, middle and last fingers bear fruit; an almost imperceptible click, and then – victory! – a segment of the box slid out from beside its neighbours.

There were two revelations.

The first, that the interior surfaces were brilliantly polished. Frank's reflection – distorted, fragmented – skated across the lacquer. The second, that Lemarchand, who had been in his time a maker of singing

3

birds, had constructed the box so that opening it tripped a musical mechanism, which began to tinkle a short rondo of sublime banality.

Encouraged by his success, Frank proceeded to work on the box more feverishly, quickly finding fresh alignments of fluted slot and oiled peg which in their turn revealed further intricacies. And with each solution – each new half twist, or pull – a further melodic element was brought into play – the tune counter-pointed and developed until the initial caprice was all but lost in ornamentation.

At some point in his labours, the bell had begun to ring – a steady sombre tolling. He had not heard it, at least not consciously. But when the puzzle was almost finished – the mirrored innards of the box unknitted – he became aware that his stomach churned so violently at the sound of the bell it might have been ringing half a lifetime.

He looked up from his work. For a few moments he supposed the noise to be coming from somewhere in the street outside – but he rapidly dismissed that notion. It had been almost midnight before he'd begun to work at the bird-maker's box; several hours had gone by – hours he would not have remembered passing but for the evidence of his watch – since then. There was no church in the city – however desperate for adherents – that would ring a summoning bell at such an hour.

No. The sound was coming from somewhere much more distant, through the very door (as yet invisible) which Lemarchand's miraculous box had been constructed to open. Everything that Kircher, who had sold him the box, had promised of it was true! He

4

was on the threshold of a new world; a province infinitely far from the room in which he sat.

Infinitely far, yet now, suddenly near.

The thought had made his breath quick. He had anticipated this moment so keenly; planned with every wit he possessed this rending of the veil. In moments they would be here – the ones Kircher had called the Cenobites, theologians of the Order of the Gash. Summoned from their experiments in the higher reaches of pleasure, to bring their ageless heads into a world of rain and failure.

He had worked ceaselessly in the preceding week to prepare the room for them. The bare boards had been meticulously scrubbed and strewn with petals. Upon the west wall he had set up a kind of altar to them, decorated with an assortment of placatory offerings Kircher had assured him would nurture their good offices: bones, bonbons, needles. A jug of his urine – the product of seven days' collection – stood on the left of the altar, should they require some spontaneous gesture of self-defilement. On the right, a plate of doves' heads, which Kircher had also advised him to have on hand.

He had left no part of the invocation ritual unobserved. No Cardinal, eager for the fisherman's shoes, could have been more diligent.

But now, as the sound of the bell became louder, drowning out the music box, he was afraid.

Too late, he murmured to himself, hoping to quell his rising fear. Lemarchand's device was undone; the final trick had been turned. There was no time left for prevarication or regret. Besides, hadn't he risked both life and sanity to make his unveiling possible?

The doorway was even now opening to pleasures no more than a handful of humans had even known existed, much less *tasted* – pleasures which would redefine the parameters of sensation, which would release him from the dull round of desire, seduction and disappointment which had dogged him from late adolescence. He would be transformed by that knowledge, wouldn't he? No man could experience the profundity of such feeling and remain unchanged.

The bare bulb in the middle of the room dimmed and brightened; brightened and dimmed again. It had taken on the rhythm of the bell, burning its hottest on each chime. In the troughs between the chimes the darkness in the room became utter; it was as if the world he had occupied for twenty-nine years had ceased to exist. Then the bell would sound again, and the bulb burn so strongly it might never have faltered, and for a few precious seconds he was standing in a familiar place, with a door that led out and down and into the street, and a window through which – had he but the will (or strength) to tear the blinds back – he might glimpse a rumour of morning.

With each peal the bulb's light was becoming more revelatory. By it, he saw the east wall flayed; saw the brick momentarily lose solidity and blow away; saw, in that same instant, the place beyond the room from which the bell's din was issuing. A world of birds, was it? Vast blackbirds caught in perpetual tempest. That was all the sense he could make of the province from which – even now – the hierophants were coming: that it was in confusion, and full of brittle, broken things that rose and fell and filled the dark air with their fright.

And then the wall was solid again, and the bell fell silent. The bulb flickered out. This time it went without a hope of rekindling.

He stood in the darkness, and said nothing. Even if he could remember the words of welcome he'd prepared, his tongue would not have spoken them. It was playing dead in his mouth.

And then, light.

It came from *them*: from the quartet of Cenobites who now, with the wall sealed behind them, occupied the room. A fitful phosphorescence came with them, like the glow of deep-sea fishes: blue, cold; charmless. It struck Frank that he had never once wondered what they look like. His imagination, though fertile when it came to trickery and theft, was impoverished in other regards: the skill to picture these eminences was beyond him, so he had not even tried.

Why then was he so distressed to set eyes upon them? Was it the scars that covered every inch of their bodies; the flesh cosmetically punctured and sliced and infibulated, then dusted down with ash? Was it the smell of vanilla they brought with them, the sweetness of which did little to disguise the stench beneath? Or was it that as the light grew, and he scanned them more closely, he saw nothing of joy, or even humanity, in their maimed faces: only desperation, and an appetite that made his bowels ache to be voided.

'What city is this?' one of the four enquired. Frank had difficulty guessing the speaker's gender with any certainty. Its clothes, some of which were sewn both *to* and *through* its skin, hid its private parts, and there was nothing in the dregs of its voice, or in its

7

wilfully disfigured features, that offered the least clue. When it spoke the hooks that transfixed the flaps on its eyes, and were wed, by an intricate system of chains passed through flesh and bone alike, to similar hooks through the lower lips, were teased by the motion, exposing the glistening meat beneath.

'I asked you a question,' it said. Frank made no reply. The name of this city was the last thing on his mind.

'Do you understand?' the figure beside the first speaker demanded. Its voice, unlike that of its companion, was light and breathy – the voice of an excited girl. Every inch of its head had been tattooed with an intricate grid, and at every intersection of horizontal and vertical axes a jewelled pin driven through to the bone. Its tongue was similarly decorated. 'Do you even know who we are?' it asked.

'Yes,' Frank said at last. 'I know.'

Of course he knew; he and Kircher had spent long nights talking of hints gleaned from the diaries of Bolingbroke and Gilles de Rais. All that mankind knew of the Order of the Gash, he knew.

And yet . . . he had expected something different. Expected some sign of the numberless splendours they had access to. He had thought they would come with women, at least; oiled women, milked women; women shaved and muscled for the act of love: their lips perfumed, their thighs trembling to spread, their buttocks weighty, the way he liked them. He had expected sighs, and languid bodies spread amongst the flowers underfoot like a living carpet; had expected virgin whores whose every crevice was his for the asking and whose skills would press him –

8

upward, upward – to undreamt-of ecstasies. The world would be forgotten in their arms. He would be exalted by his lust, instead of despised for it.

But no. No women, no sighs. Only these sexless things, with their corrugated flesh.

Now the third spoke. Its features were so heavily scarified – the wounds nurtured until they ballooned – that its eyes were invisible and its words corrupted by the disfigurement of its mouth.

'What do you want?' it asked him.

He perused this questioner more confidently than he had the other two. His fear was draining away with every second that passed. Memories of the terrifying place beyond the wall were already receding. He was left with these decrepit decadents; with their stench, their queer deformity, their self-evident frailty. The only thing he had to fear was nausea.

'Kircher told me there would be five of you,' Frank said.

'The Engineer will arrive should the moment merit,' came the reply. 'Now again, we ask you: *what do you want?*'

Why should he not answer them straight? 'Pleasure,' he replied. 'Kircher said you know about pleasure.'

'Oh we do,' said the first of them. 'Everything you ever wanted.'

'Yes?'

'Of course. Of course.' It stared at him with its all-too-naked eyes. 'What have you dreamed?' it said.

The question, put so baldly, confounded him. How could he hope to articulate the nature of the phantasms his libido had created?

He was still searching for words when one of them said: 'This world . . . it disappoints you?'

'Pretty much,' he replied.

'You're not the first to tire of its trivialities,' came the response. 'There have been others.'

'Not many,' the gridded face put in.

'True. A handful at best. But a few have dared to use Lemarchand's Configuration. Men like yourself, hungry for new possibilities, who've heard that we have skills unknown in your region.'

'I'd expected – ' Frank began.

'We know what you expected,' the Cenobite replied. 'We understand to its breadth and depth the nature of your frenzy. It is utterly familiar to us.'

Frank grunted. 'So,' he said, 'you know what I've dreamt about. You can supply the pleasure.'

The thing's face broke open, its lip curling back in a baboon's smile. 'Not as you understand it,' came the reply.

Frank made to interrupt, but the creature raised a silencing hand.

'There are conditions of the nerve-endings,' it said, 'the like of which your imagination, however fevered, could not hope to evoke.'

'. . . yes?'

'Oh yes. Oh most certainly. Your most treasured depravity is child's play beside the experiences we offer.'

'Will you partake of them?' said the second Cenobite.

Frank looked at the scars and the hooks. Again, his tongue was deficient.

'*Will you?*'

Outside, somewhere near, the world would soon be waking. He had watched it wake from the window of this very room, day after day, stirring itself to another round of fruitless pursuits, and he'd known, *known*, that there was nothing left out there to excite him. No heat, only sweat. No passion; only sudden lust, and just as sudden indifference. He had turned his back on such dissatisfaction. If in doing so he had to interpret the signs these creatures brought him, then that was the price of ambition. He was ready to pay it.

'Show me,' he said.

'There's no going back. You do understand that?'

'*Show me.*'

They needed no further invitation to raise the curtain. He heard the door creak as it was opened, and turned to see that the world beyond the threshold had disappeared, to be replaced by the same panic-filled darkness from which the members of the Order had stepped. He looked back towards the Cenobites, seeking some explanation for this. But they'd disappeared. Their passing had not gone unrecorded, however. They'd taken the flowers with them, leaving only bare boards, and on the wall the offerings he had assembled were blackening, as if in the heat of some fierce but invisible flame. He smelt the bitterness of their consumption; it pricked his nostrils so acutely he was certain they would bleed.

But the smell of burning was only the beginning. No sooner had he registered it than half a dozen other scents filled his head. Perfumes he had scarcely noticed until now were suddenly overpoweringly strong. The lingering scent of filched blossoms; the

11

smell of the paint on the ceiling and the sap in the wood beneath his feet: all filled his head.

He could even smell the darkness outside the door; and in it, the ordure of a hundred thousand birds.

He put his hand to his mouth and nose, to stop the onslaught from overcoming him, but the stench of perspiration on his fingers made him giddy. He might have been driven to nausea had there not been fresh sensations flooding his system from each nerve-ending and taste-bud.

It seemed he could suddenly feel the collision of the dust-motes with his skin. Every drawn breath chafed his lips; every blink, his eyes. Bile burned in the back of his throat, and a morsel of yesterday's beef that had lodged between his teeth sent spasms through his system as it exuded a droplet of gravy upon his tongue.

His ears were no less sensitive. His head was filled with a thousand dins, some of which he himself was father to. The air that broke against his ear-drums was a hurricane; the flatulence in his bowels was thunder. But there were other sounds – innumerable sounds – which assailed him from somewhere beyond himself. Voices raised in anger, whispered professions of love; roars and rattlings; snatches of song; tears.

Was it the world he was hearing? Morning breaking in a thousand homes? He had no chance to listen closely; the cacophony drove any power of analysis from his head.

But there was worse. The eyes! Oh God in Heaven, he had never guessed that they could be such torment; he, who'd thought there was nothing on earth left to startle him. Now he reeled! Everywhere, *sight*!

The plain plaster of the ceiling was an awesome geography of brush strokes. The weave of his plain shirt an unbearable elaboration of threads. In the corner he saw a mite move on a dead dove's head, and wink its eyes at him, seeing that he saw. Too much! *Too much*!

Appalled, he shut his eyes. But there was more *inside* than out; memories whose violence shook him to the verge of senselessness. He sucked his mother's milk, and choked; felt his sibling's arms around him (a fight was it, or a brotherly embrace? Either way, it suffocated). And more, so much more. A short lifetime of sensations, all writ in a perfect hand upon his cortex, and breaking him with their insistence that they be remembered.

He felt close to exploding. Surely the world outside his head – the room, and the birds beyond the door – they, for all their shrieking excesses, could not be as overwhelming as his memories. Better that, he thought, and tried to open his eyes. But they wouldn't unglue. Tears or pus or needle and thread had sealed them up.

He thought of the tales of the Cenobites: the hooks, the chains. Had they worked some similar surgery upon him, locking him up behind his eyes with the parade of his history?

In fear for his sanity, he began to address them, though he was no longer certain that they were even within earshot.

'*Why?*' he asked. 'Why are you doing this to me?'

The echo of his words roared in his ears, but he scarcely attended to it. More sense-impressions were swimming up from the past to torment him. Childhood still lingered on his tongue (milk and frustration) but there were adult feelings joining it now. He was grown! He was moustached and mighty; hands heavy, gut large.

Youthful pleasures had possessed the appeal of newness, but as the years had crept on, and mild sensation lost its potency, stronger and stronger experiences had been called for. And here they came again, more pungent for being laid in the darkness at the back of his head.

He felt untold tastes upon his tongue: bitter, sweet, sour, salty; smelt spice and shit and his mother's hair; saw cities and skies; saw speed, saw deeps; broke bread with men now dead and was scalded by the heat of their spittle on his cheek.

And of course there were women.

Always, amid the flurry and confusion, memories of women appeared, assaulting him with their scents, their textures, their tastes.

The proximity of this harem aroused him, despite circumstance. He opened his trousers and caressed his cock, more eager to have the seed spilt and so be freed of these creatures than for the pleasure of it.

He was dimly aware, as he worked his inches, that he must make a pitiful sight: a blind man in an empty room, aroused for a dream's sake. But the racking, joyless orgasm failed to even slow the relentless display. His knees buckled, and his body collapsed to the boards where his spunk had fallen. There was a spasm of pain as he hit the floor, but the response was washed away before another wave of memories.

He rolled on to his back, and screamed; screamed and begged for an end to it, but the sensations only rose higher still, whipped to fresh heights with every prayer for cessation he offered up.

The pleas became a single sound, words and sense eclipsed by panic. It seemed there was no end to this, but madness. No hope but to be lost to hope.

As he formulated this last, despairing thought, the torment stopped.

All at once; all of it. Gone. Sight, sound, touch, taste, smell. He was abruptly bereft of them all. There were seconds then, when he doubted his very existence. Two heartbeats; three, four.

On the fifth beat, he opened his eyes. The room was empty, the doves and piss-pot gone. The door was closed.

Gingerly, he sat up. His limbs were tingling; his head, wrist and bladder ached.

And then – a movement at the other end of the room drew his attention.

Where, two moments before, there had been an empty space, there was now a figure. It was the fourth Cenobite, the one that had never spoken, nor shown its face. Not *it* he now saw, but *she*. The hood it had worn had been discarded, as had the robes. The woman beneath was grey yet gleaming, her lips bloody, her legs parted so that the elaborate scarification of her pubis was displayed. She sat on a pile of rotting human heads, and smiled in welcome.

The collision of sensuality and death appalled him. Could he have any doubt that she had personally dispatched these victims? Their rot was beneath her nails, and their tongues – twenty or more – laid out in ranks on her oiled thighs, as if awaiting entrance. Nor did he doubt that the brains now seeping from

15

their ears and nostrils had been driven to insanity before a blow or a kiss had stopped their hearts.

Kircher had lied to him; either that or he'd been horribly deceived. There was no pleasure in the air; or at least not as humankind understood it.

He had made a mistake opening Lemarchand's box. A very terrible mistake.

'Oh, so you've finished dreaming,' said the Cenobite, perusing him as he lay panting on the bare boards. 'Good.'

She stood up. The tongues fell to the floor, like a rain of slugs.

'Now we can begin,' she said.

TWO

'It's not quite what I expected,' Julia commented as they stood in the hallway. It was twilight; a cold day in August. Not the ideal time to view a house which had been empty for so long.

'It needs work,' Rory said. 'That's all. It's not been touched since my grandmother died. That's the best part of three years. And I'm pretty sure she never did anything to it towards the end of her life.'

'And it's yours?'

'Mine and Frank's. It was willed to us both. But when was the last time anybody saw big brother . . . ?'

She shrugged, as if she couldn't remember, though she remembered very well. A week before the wedding.

'Someone said he spent a few days here last summer. Rutting away, no doubt. Then he was off again. He's got no interest in property.'

'But suppose we move in, and then he comes back; wants what's his?'

'I'll buy him out. I'll get a loan from the bank and buy him out. He's always hard up for cash.'

She nodded, but looked less than persuaded.

'Don't worry,' he said, going to where she was standing and wrapping his arms around her. 'The

17

place is ours, doll. We can paint it and pamper it and make it like Heaven.'

He scanned her face. Sometimes – particularly when doubt moved her as it did now – her beauty came close to frightening him.

'Trust me,' he said.

'I do.'

'All right then. What say we start moving in on Sunday?'

2

Sunday.

It was still the Lord's Day up this end of the city. Even if the owners of these well-dressed houses and well-pressed children were no longer believers, they still observed the Sabbath. A few curtains were twitched aside when Lewton's van drew up, and the unloading began; some curious neighbours even sauntered past the house once or twice, on the pretext of walking the hounds; but nobody spoke to the new arrivals, much less offered a hand with the furniture. Sunday was not a day to break sweat.

Julia looked after the unpacking, while Rory organized the unloading of the van, with Lewton and Mad Bob providing the extra muscle. It took four round trips to transfer the bulk of the stuff from Alexandra Road, and at the end of the day there was still a good deal of bric-a-brac left behind, to be collected at a later point.

About two in the afternoon, Kirsty turned up on the doorstep.

'Came to see if I could give you a hand,' she said, with a tone of vague apology in her voice.

'Well, you'd better come in,' Julia said. She went back into the front room, which was a battlefield in which only chaos was winning, and quietly cursed Rory. Inviting the lost soul round to offer her services was his doing, no doubt of it. She would be more of a hindrance than a help; her dreamy, perpetually defeated manner set Julia's teeth on edge.

'What can I do?' Kirsty asked. 'Rory said – '

'Yes,' said Julia. 'I'm sure he did.'

'Where is he? Rory, I mean.'

'Gone back for another van-load, to add to the misery.'

'Oh.'

Julia softened her expression. 'You know it's very sweet of you,' she said, 'to come round like this, but I don't think there's much you can do just at the moment.'

Kirsty flushed slightly. Dreamy she was; but not stupid.

'I see,' she said. 'Are you sure? Can't . . . I mean, maybe I could make a cup of coffee for you?'

'Coffee,' said Julia. The thought of it made her realize just how parched her throat had become. 'Yes,' she conceded. 'That's not a bad idea.'

The coffee-making was not without its minor traumas. No task Kirsty undertook was ever entirely simple. She stood in the kitchen, boiling water in a pan it had taken a quarter of an hour to find, thinking that maybe she shouldn't have come after all. Julia always looked at her so strangely, as if faintly baffled by the fact she hadn't been smothered at birth. No matter. *Rory* had asked her to come, hadn't he? And that was invitation enough. She would not have turned down the chance of his smile for a hundred Julias.

The van arrived twenty-five minutes later; minutes in which the women had twice attempted, and twice failed, to get a conversation simmering. They had little in common: Julia the sweet, the beautiful, the winner of glances and kisses, and Kirsty the girl with the pale handshake, whose eyes were only ever as bright as Julia's before or after tears. She had long ago decided that life was unfair. But why, when she'd accepted that bitter truth, did circumstance insist on rubbing her face in it?

She surreptitiously watched Julia as she worked, and it seemed to Kirsty that the woman was incapable of ugliness. Every gesture – a stray hair brushed from the eyes with the back of the hand, dust blown from a favourite cup – all were infused with such effortless grace. Seeing it, she understood Rory's dog-like adulation; and understanding it, despaired afresh.

He came in, at last, squinting and sweaty. The afternoon sun was fierce. He grinned at her, parading the ragged line of his front teeth that she had first found so irresistible.

'I'm glad you could come,' he said.

'Happy to help – ' she replied, but he had already looked away: at Julia.

'How's it going?'

'I'm losing my mind,' she told him.

'Well now you can rest from your labours,' he said. 'We brought the bed this trip.' He gave her a conspiratorial wink, but she didn't respond.

'Can I help with unloading?' Kirsty offered.

'Lewton and M.B. are doing it,' came Rory's reply.

'Oh.'

'But I'd give an arm and a leg for a cup of tea.'

'We haven't found the tea,' Julia told him.

'Oh. Maybe a coffee, then?'

'Right,' said Kirsty. 'And for the other two?'

'They'd kill for a cup.'

Kirsty went back to the kitchen, filled the small pan to near brimming, and set it back on the stove. From the hallway she heard Rory supervising the next unloading.

It was the bed; the bridal bed. Though she tried very hard to keep the thought of his embracing Julia out of her mind, she could not. As she stared into the water, and it simmered and steamed and finally boiled, the same painful images of their pleasure came back and back.

3

While the trio were away, gathering the fourth and final load of the day, Julia lost her temper with the unpacking. It was a disaster, she said; everything had been parcelled up and put into the tea chests in the wrong order. She was having to disinter perfectly useless items to get access to the bare necessities.

Kirsty kept her silence, and her place in the kitchen, washing the soiled cups.

Cursing louder, Julia left the chaos and went out for a cigarette on the front step. She leaned against the open door, and breathed the pollen-gilded air. Already, though it was only the 21st of August, the afternoon was tinged with a smoky scent that heralded autumn.

She had lost track of how fast the day had gone, for as she stood there a bell began to ring for Evensong: the run of chimes rising and falling in lazy waves. The sound was reassuring. It made her think of her childhood, though not – that she could remember – of any particular day or place. Simply of being young; of mystery.

It was four years since she'd last stepped into a church: the day of her marriage to Rory, in fact. The thought of that day – or rather of the promise it had failed to fulfil – soured the moment. She left the step, the chimes in full flight, and turned back into the house. After the touch of the sun on her upturned face, the interior seemed gloomy. Suddenly she was tired to the point of tears.

They would have to assemble the bed before they could put their heads down to sleep tonight, and they had yet to decide which room they would use as the master bedroom. She would do that now, she elected, and so avoid having to return to the front room, and to ever-mournful Kirsty.

The bell was still pealing when she opened the door of the front room on the second floor. It was the largest of the three upper rooms – a natural choice – but the sun had not got in today (or any other day this summer) because the blinds were drawn across the window. The room was consequently chillier than anywhere else in the house; the air stagnant. She crossed the stained floorboards to the window, intending to remove the blind.

At the sill, a strange thing. The blind had been securely nailed to the window-frame, effectively cutting out the least intrusion of life from the sunlit street beyond. She tried to pull the material free, but failed. The workman, whoever he'd been, had done a thorough job.

No matter, she'd have Rory take a claw-hammer to the nails when he got back. She turned from the window, and as she did so she was suddenly and forcibly aware that the bell was still summoning the faithful. Were they not coming tonight? Was the hook not sufficiently baited with promises of paradise? The thought was only half alive; it withered in moments. But the bell rolled on, reverberating around the room. Her limbs, already aching with fatigue, seemed dragged down further by each peal. Her head throbbed intolerably.

The room was hateful, she'd decided; it was stale, and its benighted walls clammy. Despite its size, she would not let Rory persuade her into using it as the master bedroom. Let it rot.

She started towards the door, but as she came within a yard of it, the corners of the room seemed to creak, and the door slammed. Her nerves jangled. It was all she could do to prevent herself from sobbing.

Instead she simply said: 'Go to hell,' and snatched at the handle. It turned easily (why should it not?;

yet she was relieved) and the door swung open. From the hall below, a splash of warmth and ochre light.

She closed the door behind her and, with a queer satisfaction the root of which she couldn't or wouldn't fathom, turned the key in the lock.

As she did so, the bell stopped.

4

'But it's the biggest of the rooms . . .'

'I don't like it, Rory. It's damp. We can use the back room.'

'If we can get the bloody bed through the door.'

'Of course we can. You know we can.'

'Seems a waste of a good room,' he protested, knowing full well that this was a *fait accompli*.

'Mother knows best,' she told him, and smiled at him with eyes whose lustre was far from maternal.

THREE

The seasons long for each other, like men and women, in order that they may be cured of their excesses.

Spring, if it lingers more than a week beyond its span, starts to hunger for summer to end the days of perpetual promise. Summer in its turn soon begins to sweat for something to quench its heat, and the mellowest of autumns will tire of gentility at last, and ache for a quick sharp frost to kill its fruitfulness.

Even winter – the hardest season, the most implacable – dreams, as February creeps on, of the flame that will presently melt it away. Everything tires with time, and starts to seek some opposition, to save it from itself.

So August gave way to September and there were few complaints.

2

With work, the house on Lodovico Street began to look more hospitable. There were even visits from neighbours, who – after sizing up the couple – spoke freely of how happy they were to have number fifty-five occupied again. Only one of them made any mention of Frank, referring in passing to the odd fellow who'd lived in the house for a few weeks the previous summer. There was a moment of embarrassment when Rory revealed the tenant to have been his brother, but it was soon glossed over by Julia, whose power to charm knew no bounds.

Rory had seldom made mention of Frank during the years of his marriage to Julia, though he and his brother were only eighteen months apart in age, and as children had been inseparable. This Julia had learned on an occasion of drunken reminiscing – a month or two before the wedding – when Rory had spoken at length about Frank. It had been melancholy talk. The brothers' paths had diverged considerably once they'd passed through adolescence, and Rory regretted it. Regretted still more the pain Frank's wild life-style had brought to their parents. It seemed that when Frank appeared, once in a blue moon, from whichever corner of the globe he was presently laying waste, he only brought grief. His tales of adventures in the shallows of criminality, his talk of whores and petty theft, all appalled the family. But there had been worse, or so Rory had said. In his wilder moments Frank had talked of life lived in delirium; of an appetite for experience that conceded no moral imperative.

Was it the tone of Rory's telling, a mixture of revulsion and envy, that had so piqued Julia's curiosity? Whatever the reason, she had been quickly seized by an unquenchable curiosity concerning this madman.

26

Then, barely a fortnight before the wedding, the black sheep had appeared in the flesh. Things had gone well for him of late. He was wearing gold rings on his fingers, and his skin was tight and tanned. There was little outward sign of the monster Rory had described. Brother Frank was smooth as a polished stone. She had succumbed to his charm within hours.

A strange time ensued. As the days crept towards the date of the wedding she found herself thinking less and less of her husband to be, and more and more of his brother. They were not wholly dissimilar; a certain lilt in their voices, and their easy manner, marked them as siblings. But to Rory's qualities Frank brought something his brother would never have: a beautiful desperation.

Perhaps what had happened next had been inevitable; and no matter how hard she'd fought her instincts, she would only have postponed the consummation of their feelings for each other. At least that was how she tried to excuse herself later. But when all the self-recrimination was done with she still treasured the memory of their first – and last – encounter.

Kirsty had been at the house, hadn't she, on some matrimonial business, when Frank had arrived. But by that telepathy which comes with desire (and fades with it) Julia had known that today was the day. She'd left Kirsty to her list-making or suchlike, and taken Frank upstairs on the pretext of showing him the wedding dress. That was how she remembered it; that he'd asked to see the dress, and she'd put the veil on, laughing to think of herself in white, and then he'd been at her shoulder, lifting the veil, and she'd laughed on, laughed and laughed, as though to test the strength of his purpose. He had not been cooled by her mirth however, nor had he wasted time with the niceties of a seduction. The smooth exterior gave way to cruder stuff almost immediately. Their coupling had had, in every regard but the matter of her acquiescence, all the aggression and the joylessness of rape.

Memory sweetened events, of course, and in the four years (and five months) since that afternoon, she'd replayed the scene often. Now, in remembering it, the bruises were trophies of their passion; her tears proof positive of her feelings for him.

The day following, he'd disappeared. Flitted off to Bangkok or Easter Island, some place where he had no debts to answer. She'd mourned him; couldn't help it. Nor had her mourning gone unnoticed. Though it was never explicitly discussed, she had often wondered if the subsequent deterioration of her relationship with Rory had not started there: with her thinking of Frank as she made love to his brother.

And now? Now, despite the change of domestic interiors, and the chance of a fresh start together, it seemed that events conspired to remind her again of Frank.

It wasn't just the gossip of the neighbours that brought him to mind. One day, when she was alone in the house, and unpacking various personal belongings, she came across several wallets of Rory's photographs. Many were relatively recent pictures of the two of them together in Athens and Malta. But buried amongst the transparent smiles were some

28

pictures she couldn't remember ever having seen before (had Rory kept them from her?); family portraits that went back decades. A photograph of his parents on their wedding day; the black and white image eroded over the years to a series of greys. Pictures of christenings, in which proud godparents cradled babies smothered in the family lace.

And then, photographs of the brothers together; as toddlers, with wide eyes; as surly schoolchildren, snapped at gymnastic displays and in school pageants. Then, as the shyness of acne-ridden adolescence took over, the number of pictures dwindled – until the frogs emerged, as princes, the other side of puberty.

Seeing Frank in brilliant colour, clowning for the camera, she felt herself blushing. He had been an exhibitionist youth, predictably enough; always dressed *à la mode*. Rory, by comparison, looked dowdy. It seemed to her that the brothers' future lives were sketched in these early portraits. Frank the smiling, seductive chameleon; Rory the solid citizen.

She had packed the pictures away at last, and found, when she stood up, that with the blushes had come tears. Not of regret. She had no use for that. It was *fury* which made her eyes sting. Somehow, between one breath and the next, she'd lost herself.

She knew too, with perfect certainty, when her grip had first faltered. Lying on a bed of wedding lace, while Frank beset her neck with kisses.

29

3

Once in a while she went up to the room with the sealed blinds.

So far, they'd done little decorating work on the upper floors, preferring to first organize the areas in public gaze. The room had therefore remained untouched. *Unentered*, indeed, except for these few visits of hers.

She wasn't sure why she went up; nor how to account for the odd assortment of feelings that beset her while there. But there was something about the dark interior which gave her comfort: it was a womb of sorts; a dead woman's womb. Sometimes, when Rory was at work, she simply took herself up the stairs and sat in the stillness thinking of nothing; or at least nothing she could put words to.

These sojourns made her feel oddly guilty, and she tried to stay away from the room when Rory was around. But it wasn't always possible. Sometimes her feet took her there without instructions so to do.

It happened thus that Saturday, the day of the blood.

She had been watching Rory at work on the kitchen door, chiselling several layers of paint around the hinges, when she seemed to hear the room call. Satisfied that he was thoroughly engrossed in his chores, she went upstairs.

It was cooler than usual, and she was glad of it.

She put her hand to the wall, and then transferred her chilled palm to her forehead.

'No use,' she murmured to herself, picturing the man at work downstairs. She didn't love him; no more than he, beneath his infatuation with her face, loved her. He chiselled in a world of his own; she suffered here, far removed from him.

A gust of wind caught the back door below. She heard it slam.

Downstairs, the sound made Rory lose his concentration. The chisel jumped its groove and sliced deeply into the thumb of his left hand. He shouted, as a gush of colour came. The chisel hit the floor.

'Hell and damnation!'

She heard, but did nothing. Too late, she surfaced through a stupor of melancholy to realize that he was coming upstairs. Fumbling for the key, and an excuse to justify her presence in the room, she stood up, but he was already at the door, crossing the threshold, rushing towards her, his right hand clamped ineptly around his left. Blood was coming in abundance. It welled up between his fingers and dribbled down his arm, dripping from his elbow, adding stain to stain on the bare boards.

'What have you done?' she asked him.

'What does it look like?' he said through gritted teeth. 'Cut myself.'

His face and neck had gone the colour of window-putty. She'd seen him like this before, he had on occasion passed out at the sight of his own blood.

'Do something,' he said queasily.

'Is it deep?'

31

'I don't know!' he yelled at her. 'I don't want to look.'

He was ridiculous, she thought; but this wasn't the time to give vent to the contempt she felt. Instead she took his bloody hand in hers and, while he looked away, prised the palm from the cut. It was sizeable, and still bleeding profusely. Deep blood; dark blood.

'I think we'd better take you off to the hospital,' she told him.

'Can you cover it up?' he asked, his voice devoid of anger now.

'Sure. I'll get a clean binding. Come on – '

'No,' he said, shaking his ashen face. 'If I take a step, I think I'll pass out.'

'Stay here then,' she soothed him. 'You'll be fine.'

Finding no bandages in the bathroom cabinet the equal of the staunching, she fetched a few clean handkerchiefs from his drawer and went back into the room. He was leaning against the wall now, his skin glossy with sweat. He had padded in the blood he'd shed; she could taste the tang of it in the air.

Still quietly reassuring him that he wouldn't die of a two-inch cut, she wound a handkerchief around his hand, bound it on with a second, then escorted him, trembling like a leaf, down the stairs (one by one, like a child) and out to the car.

At the hospital they waited an hour in a queue of the walking wounded before he was finally seen and stitched up. It was difficult for her to know in retrospect what was more comical about the episode: his weakness, or the extravagance of his subsequent gratitude. She told him, when he became too fulsome, that she didn't want thanks from him, and it was true.

She wanted nothing that he could offer her, except perhaps his absence.

4

'Did you clean up the floor in the damp room?' she asked him the following day. They'd called it the damp room since that first Sunday, though there was not a sign of rot from ceiling to skirting board.

Rory looked up from his magazine. Grey moons hung beneath his eyes. He hadn't slept well, so he'd said. A cut finger, and he had nightmares of mortality. She, on the other hand, had slept like a babe.

'What did you say?' he asked her.

'The floor,' she said again. 'There was blood on the floor. You cleaned it up.'

He shook his head. 'No,' he said simply, and returned to the magazine.

'Well I didn't,' she said.

He offered her an indulgent smile. 'You're such a perfect *hausfrau*,' he said. 'You don't even know when you're doing it.'

The subject was closed there. He was content, apparently, to believe that she was quietly losing her sanity.

She, on the other hand, had the strangest sense that she was about to find it again.

FOUR

Kirsty hated parties. The smiles to be pasted on over the panic; the glances to be interpreted; and worst, the conversation. She had nothing to say of the least interest to the world, of this she had long been convinced. She'd watched too many eyes glaze over to believe otherwise; seen every device known to man for wheedling oneself out of the company of the dull, from: 'Will you excuse me, I believe I see my accountant', to passing out dead drunk at her feet.

But Rory had insisted she come to the house-warming. Just a few close friends, he'd promised. She'd said yes, knowing all too well what scenario would ensue her from refusal. Moping at home in a stew of self-recrimination, cursing her cowardice and thinking of Rory's sweet face.

The gathering wasn't such a torment, as it turned out. There were only nine guests *in toto*, all of whom she knew vaguely, which made it easier. They didn't expect her to illuminate the room; only to nod and laugh where appropriate. And Rory — his hand still bound up — was at his most winning, full of guileless *bonhomie*. She even wondered if Neville — one of Rory's work colleagues — wasn't making eyes at her behind his spectacles, a suspicion which was confirmed in the middle of the evening when he manoeuvred himself to her side and enquired whether she had any interest in cat-breeding. She told him she hadn't, but was always interested in new experiences. He seemed delighted, and on this fragile pretext proceeded to ply her with liqueurs for the rest of the night. By eleven-thirty she was a whoozy but happy wreck, prompted by the most casual remark to ever more painful fits of giggling.

A little after midnight, Julia declared that she was tired, and wanted to go to bed. The statement was taken as a general cue for dispersal, but Rory would have none of it. He was up and re-filling glasses before anyone had a chance to protest. Kirsty was certain she caught a look of displeasure cross Julia's face, then it passed, and the brow was unsullied once again. She said her goodnights, was complimented profusely on her skill with calf's liver, and went to bed.

The flawlessly beautiful were flawlessly happy, weren't they? To Kirsty this had always seemed self-evident. Tonight, however, the alcohol made her wonder if envy hadn't blinded her. Perhaps to be flawless was another kind of sadness.

But her spinning head had an inept hold on such ruminations, and the next minute Rory was up, and telling a joke about a gorilla and a Jesuit which had her choking on her drink before he'd even got to the votive candles.

Upstairs, Julia heard a fresh bout of laughter. She was indeed tired, as she'd claimed, but it wasn't the cooking that had exhausted her. It was the effort of suppressing her contempt for the damn fools who were gathered in the lounge below. She'd called them friends once, these halfwits, with their poor jokes and their poorer pretensions. She had played along with them for several hours; it was enough. Now she needed some cool place; some darkness.

As soon as she opened the door of the damp room she knew things were not quite as they had been. The light from the shadeless bulb on the landing illuminated the boards where Rory's blood had fallen, now so clean they might have been scrubbed. Beyond the reach of the light, the room bowed to darkness. She stepped in, and closed the door. The lock clicked into place at her back.

The dark was almost perfect, and she was glad of it. Her eyes rested against the night, their surfaces chilled.

Then, from the far side of the room, she heard a sound.

It was no louder than the din of a cockroach running behind the skirting boards. After seconds, it stopped. She held her breath. It came again. This time there seemed to be some pattern to the sound; a primitive code.

They were laughing like loons downstairs. The noise awoke desperation in her. What would she not do, to be free of such company?

She swallowed, and spoke to the darkness.

'I hear you,' she said, not certain of why the words came, or to whom they were addressed.

The cockroach scratches ceased for a moment, and then began again, more urgently. She stepped away from the door and moved towards the noise. It continued, as if summoning her.

It was easy to miscalculate in the dark, and she reached the wall before she'd expected to. Raising her hands, she began to run her palms over the painted plaster. The surface was not uniformly cold. There was a place, she judged it to be halfway between door and window, where the chill became so intense she had to break contact. The cockroach stopped scratching.

There was a moment when she swam, totally disoriented, in darkness and silence. And then something moved in front of her. A trick of her mind's eye, she assumed, for there was only imagined light to be had here. But the next spectacle showed her the error of that assumption.

The wall was alight; or rather something behind it burned with a cold luminescence which made the solid brick seem insubstantial stuff. *More*: the wall seemed to be coming apart, segments of it shifting and dislocating like a magician's prop, oiled panels giving on to hidden boxes whose sides in turn collapsed to reveal some further hiding place. She watched fixedly, not daring even to blink for fear she miss some detail of this extraordinary sleight-of-hand, while pieces of the world came apart in front of her eyes.

Then, suddenly, somewhere in this ever more elaborate system of sliding fragments, she saw (or again, *seemed* to see) movement. Only now did she realize that she'd been holding her breath since this display began, and was beginning to become lightheaded. She tried to empty her lungs of the stale air, and take a draught of fresh, but her body would not obey this simple instruction.

Somewhere in her innards a tic of panic began. The hocus-pocus had stopped now, leaving one part of her admiring quite dispassionately the tinkling music which was coming from the wall, the other part fighting the fear that rose in her throat step by step.

Again, she tried to take a breath, but it was as if her body had died, and she was staring out of it, unable now to breathe or blink or swallow.

The spectacle of the unfolding wall had now ceased entirely and she saw something flicker across the brick; ragged enough to be shadow but too substantial.

It was human, she saw, or had been. But the body had been ripped apart and sewn together again with most of its pieces either missing or twisted and blackened as if in a furnace. There was an eye, gleaming at her, and the ladder of a spine, the vertebrae stripped of muscle; a few unrecognizable fragments of anatomy. That was it. That such a thing might live beggared reason – what little flesh it owned was hopelessly corrupted. Yet live it did. Its eye, despite the rot it was rooted in, scanned her every inch, up and down.

She felt no fear in its presence. The thing was weaker than her by far. It moved a little in its cell, looking for some modicum of comfort. But there was none to be had; not for a creature that wore its frayed nerves on its bleeding sleeve. Every place it might lay its body brought pain: this she knew indisputably. She pitied it. And with pity came release. Her body expelled dead air, and sucked in living. Her oxygen-starved brain reeled.

Even as she did so it spoke, a hole opening up in the flayed ball of the monster's head and issuing a single, weightless word.

The word was: 'Julia.'

2

Kirsty put down her glass, and tried to stand up.

'Where are you going?' Neville asked her.

'Where do you think?' she replied, consciously trying to prevent the words from slurring.

'Do you need any help?' Rory inquired. The alcohol made his lids lazy, and his grin lazier still.

'I am house-trained,' she replied, the riposte greeted with laughter all round. She was pleased with herself; off-the-cuff wit was not her forte. She stumbled to the door.

'It's the last room on the right at the end of the landing,' Rory informed her.

'I know,' she said, and stepped out into the hall.

She didn't usually enjoy the sensation of drunkenness, but tonight she was revelling in it. She felt loose-limbed and light-hearted. She might well regret this tomorrow, but tomorrow would have to take care of itself. For tonight, she was flying.

She found her way to the bathroom, and relieved her aching bladder, then splashed some water on to her face. That done, she began her return journey.

She had taken three steps along the landing when she realized that somebody had put out the landing light while she was in the bathroom, and that same somebody was now standing a few yards away from her. She stopped.

'Hello . . . ?' she said. Had the cat-breeder followed her upstairs, in the hope of proving he wasn't spayed?

'Is that you?' she asked, only dimly aware that this was a singularly fruitless line of enquiry.

There was no reply, and she became a little uneasy.

'Come on,' she said, attempting a jocular manner that she hoped masked her anxiety, 'who is it?'

'Me,' said Julia. Her voice was odd. Throaty; perhaps tearful.

'Are you all right?' Kirsty asked her. She wished she could see Julia's face.

'Yes,' came the reply. 'Why shouldn't I be?' Within the space of those five words the actress in Julia seized control. The voice cleared; the tone lightened.

'I'm just tired . . .' she went on. 'It sounds like you're having a good time down there.'

'Are we keeping you awake?'

'Goodness me, no,' the voice gushed, 'I was just going to the bathroom.' A pause, then: 'You go back down. Enjoy yourself.'

At this cue Kirsty moved towards her along the landing. At the last possible moment Julia stepped out of the way, avoiding even the slightest physical contact.

'Sleep well,' Kirsty said at the top of the stairs.

But there was no reply forthcoming from the shadow on the landing.

Julia didn't sleep well. Not that night, nor any night that followed.

What she'd seen in the damp room, what she'd heard and, finally, *felt* – was enough to keep easy slumbers at bay forever; or so she began to believe.

He was here. Brother Frank was here, in the house – and had been all the time. Locked away from the world in which she lived and breathed, but close enough to make the frail, pitiful contact he had. The whys and the wherefores of this she had no clue to; the human detritus in the wall had neither the strength nor the time to articulate its condition.

All it said, before the wall began to close on it again, and its wreckage was once more eclipsed by brick and plaster, was *'Julia'* – then, simply: *'It's Frank'* – and at the very end the word *'Blood'*.

Then it was gone completely, and her legs had given way beneath her. She'd half fallen, half staggered, backwards against the opposite wall. By the time she gathered her wits about her once more there was no mysterious light; no wasted figure cocooned in the brick. Reality's hold was absolute once again.

Not *quite* absolute perhaps. Frank was still here, in the damp room. Of that she had no doubt. Out of sight he might be, but not out of mind. He was trapped somehow between the sphere she occupied and some other place: a place of bells and troubled darkness. Had he died, was that it? Perished in the empty room the previous summer, and his spirit left there awaiting exorcism? If so, what had happened to his earthly remains? Only further exchange with Frank himself, or the remains thereof, would provide an explanation.

Of the means by which she could lend the lost soul strength she had little doubt. He had given her the solution plainly.

Blood, he'd said. The syllable had been spoken not as an accusation but as an imperative.

Rory had bled on the floor of the damp room; the splash had subsequently disappeared. Somehow, Frank's ghost – if that it was – had fed upon his brother's spillage, and gained thereby nourishment enough to reach out from his cell, and make faltering contact. What more might be achieved if the supply were larger?

She thought of Frank's embraces; of his roughness, his hardness; of the insistence he had brought to bear upon her. What would she not give to have such insistence again? Perhaps it was possible. And if it were – if she could give him the sustenance he needed – would he not be grateful? Would he not be her pet; docile or brutal at her least whim? The thought took sleep away. Took sanity and sorrow with it. She had been in love all this time, she realized, and mourning for him. If it took blood to restore him to her, then blood she would supply, and not think twice of the consequences.

In the days that followed, she found her smile again.

Rory took the change of mood as a sign that she was happy in the new house. Her good humour ignited the same in him. He took to the re-decoration with renewed gusto.

Soon, he said, he would get to work on the second floor. They would locate the source of dampness in the large room, and turn it into a bedroom fit for his princess. She kissed his cheek when he spoke of this, and said that she was in no hurry: that the room they had already was more than adequate. Talk of the bedroom made him stroke her neck, and pull her close, and whisper infantile obscenities in her ear. She did not refuse him, but went upstairs meekly, and let him undress her as he liked to do, unbuttoning her with paint-stained fingers. She pretended the ceremony aroused her, though this was far from the truth.

The only thing that sparked the least appetite in her, as she lay on the creaking bed with his bulk between her legs, was closing her eyes and picturing Frank, as he had been.

More than once his name rose to her lips; each time she bit it back. Finally she opened her eyes to remind herself of the boorish truth. Rory was decorating her face with his kisses. Her cheeks crawled at his touch.

She would not be able to endure this too often, she realized. It was too much of an effort to play the acquiescent wife: her heart would burst.

Thus, lying beneath him while September's breath brushed her face from the open window, she began to plot the getting of blood.

FIVE

Sometimes it seemed that aeons came and went while he lingered in the wall; aeons that some clue would later reveal to have been the passing of hours, or even minutes.

But now things had changed; he had a chance of *escape*. His spirit soared at the thought of it. It was a frail chance; he didn't deceive himself about that. There were several reasons his best efforts might falter. Julia, for one. He remembered her as a trite, preening woman, whose upbringing had curbed her capacity for passion. He had untamed her, of course; once. He remembered the day, amongst the thousands of times he had performed that act, with some satisfaction. She had resisted no more than was needful for her vanity, then succumbed with such naked fervour he had almost lost control of himself.

In other circumstances he might have snatched her from under her would-be husband's nose, but fraternal politics counselled otherwise. In a week or two he would have tired of her, and been left not only with a woman whose body was already an eyesore to him, but a vengeful brother on his heels. It hadn't been worth the hassle.

Besides, there'd been new worlds to conquer. He had left the day after to go East: to Hong Kong and

Sri Lanka; to wealth and adventure. He'd had them, too. At least for a while. But everything slipped through his fingers sooner or later, and with time he began to wonder whether it was circumstance that denied him a good hold on his earnings, or whether he simply didn't care enough to keep what he had. The train of thought, once begun, was a runaway. Everywhere, in the wreckage around him, he found evidence to support the same bitter thesis: that he had encountered nothing in his life – no person, no state of mind or body – he wanted sufficiently to suffer even passing discomfort for.

A downward spiral began. He spent three months in a wash of depression and self-pity that bordered on the suicidal. But even that solution was denied him by his new-found nihilism. If nothing was worth living for it followed, didn't it, that there was nothing worth dying for either. He stumbled from one such sterility to the next, until all thoughts were rotted away by whatever opiate his immoralities could earn him.

How had he first heard about Lemarchand's box? He couldn't remember. In a bar maybe; or a gutter, from the lips of a fellow derelict. At the time it was merely a rumour – this dream of a pleasure dome where those who had exhausted the trivial delights of the human condition might discover a fresh definition of joy. And the route to this paradise? There were several, he was told, charts of the interface between the real and the realer still, made by travellers whose bones had long since gone to dust. One such chart was in the vaults of the Vatican, hidden in code in a theological work unread since the Reformation. Another, in the form of an origami exercise, was reported to have been in the possession of the Marquis de Sade, who had used it, while imprisoned in the Bastille, to barter with a guard for paper on which to write *The 120 Days of Sodom*. Yet another was made by a craftsman – a maker of singing birds – called Lemarchand, in the form of a musical box of such elaborate design a man might toy with it half a lifetime and never get inside.

Stories. Stories. Yet since he had come to believe in nothing at all it was not so difficult to put the tyranny of verifiable truth out of his head. And it passed the time, musing drunkenly on such fantasies.

It was in Düsseldorf, where he'd gone smuggling heroin, that he again encountered the story of Lemarchand's box. His curiosity was piqued once more; but this time he followed up the story until he found its source. The man's name was Kircher, though he probably laid claim to half a dozen others. Yes, the German could confirm the existence of the box; and yes, he could see his way to letting Frank have it. The price? Small favours, here and there. Nothing exceptional. Frank did the favours, washed his hands, and claimed his payment.

There had been instructions from Kircher, on how best to break the seal on Lemarchand's device; instructions that were part pragmatic, part metaphysical. To solve the puzzle is to travel, he'd said; or something like that. The box, it seemed, was not just the map of the road, but the road itself.

This new addiction quickly cured him of dope and drink. Perhaps there were other ways to bend the world to suit the shape of his dreams.

He came back to the house on Lodovico Street, to the empty house behind whose walls he was now imprisoned, and prepared himself – just as Kircher had detailed – for the challenge of solving Lemarchand's Configuration. He had never in his life been so abstemious, nor so single-minded. In the days before the onslaught on the box he led a life which would have shamed a saint, focusing all his energies on the ceremonies ahead.

He had been arrogant in his dealing with the Order of the Gash, he saw that now; but there were everywhere – *in* the world and *out* of it – forces that encouraged such arrogance because they traded on it. That in itself would not have undone him. No; his real error had been the naïve belief that *his* definition of pleasure significantly overlapped with that of the Cenobites.

As it was, they had brought incalculable suffering. They had overdosed him on sensuality, until his mind teetered on madness, then they'd initiated him into experiences that his nerves still convulsed to recall. They called it pleasure; and perhaps they'd meant it. Perhaps not. It was impossible to know with these minds; they were so hopelessly, flawlessly ambiguous. They recognized no principles of reward and punishment by which he could hope to win some respite from their tortures, nor were they touched by any appeal for mercy. He'd tried that, over the weeks and months that separated the solving of the box from today.

There was no compassion to be had on this side of the Schism; there was only the weeping and the laughter. Tears of joy sometimes (for an hour without dread; a breath's length even); laughter coming just as paradoxically in the face of some new horror, fashioned by the Engineer for the provision of grief.

There was a further sophistication to the torture, devised by a mind that understood exquisitely the nature of suffering. The prisoners were allowed to see into the world they had once occupied. Their resting places – when they were not enduring pleasure – looked out on to the very locations where they had once worked the Configuration that had brought them here. In Frank's case, on to the upper room of number fifty-five, Lodovico Street.

For the best part of a year it had been an unilluminating view; nobody had even stepped into the house. And then, *they*'d come: Rory and the lovely Julia. And hope had begun again . . .

There were ways to escape, he'd heard it whispered; loopholes in the system that might allow a mind supple or cunning enough egress into the room from which it had come. If a prisoner were able to make such an escape, there was no way that the hierophants could follow. They had to be *summoned* across the Schism. Without such an invitation they were left like dogs on the doorstep, scratching and scratching but unable to get in. Escape therefore, if it could be achieved, brought with it a *decree absolute*, total dissolution of the mistaken marriage which the prisoner had made. It was a risk worth taking. Indeed it was no risk at all. What punishment could be meted out worse than the thought of pain without hope of release?

He had been lucky. Some prisoners had departed from the world without leaving sufficient sign of themselves from which, given an adequate collision of circumstances, their bodies might be remade. He had. Almost his last act, bar the shouting, had been to empty his testicles on to the floor. Dead sperm was a meagre keepsake of his essential self: but enough. When dear brother Rory (sweet butter-fingered Rory) had let his chisel slip, there was something of Frank to profit from the pain. He had found a finger-hold for himself, and a glimpse of strength with which he might haul himself to safety. Now it was up to Julia.

Sometimes, suffering in the wall, he thought she would desert him out of fear. Either that or she'd rationalize the vision she'd seen, and decide she'd been dreaming. If so, he was lost. He lacked the energy to repeat the appearance.

But there were signs that gave him cause for hope. The fact that she returned to the room on two or three occasions, for instance, and simply stood in the gloom, watching the wall. She'd even muttered a few words on the second visit, though he'd caught only scraps. The word 'here' was amongst them. And 'waiting'; and 'soon'. Enough to keep him from despair.

He had another prop to his optimism. She was lost, wasn't she? He'd seen that in her face, when — before the day Rory had chiselled himself — she and his brother had had occasion to be in the room together. He'd read the looks between the lines; the moments when her guard had slipped, and the sadness and frustration she felt were apparent.

Yes, she was lost. Married to a man she felt no love for, and unable to see a way out.

Well, here he was. They could save each other, the way the poets promised lovers should. He was mystery, he was darkness, he was all she had dreamt of. And if she would only free him he would service her – oh yes – until her pleasure reached that threshold that, like all thresholds, was a place where the strong grew stronger, and the weak perished.

Pleasure was pain there; and vice versa. And he knew it well enough to call it home.

SIX

It turned cold in the third week of September: an arctic chill brought on a rapacious wind that stripped the trees of leaves in a handful of days.

The cold necessitated a change of costume, and a change of plan. Instead of walking, Julia took the car. Drove down to the city centre in the early afternoon and found a bar in which the lunchtime trade was brisk but not clamorous.

The customers came and went; young turks from firms of lawyers and accountants, debating their ambitions; parties of wine-imbibers whose only claim to sobriety was their suits; and, more interestingly, a smattering of individuals who sat alone at their tables and simply drank. She garnered a good crop of admiring glances, but they were mostly from the young turks. It wasn't until she'd been in the place an hour, and the wage-slaves were returning to their tread-mills, that she caught sight of somebody watching her reflection in the bar mirror. For the next ten minutes his eyes were glued to her. She went on drinking, trying to conceal any sign of agitation. And then, without warning, he stood up and crossed to her table.

'Drinking alone?' he said.

She wanted to run. Her heart was pounding so

furiously she was certain he must hear it. But no. He asked her if she wanted another drink; she said she did. Clearly pleased not to have been rebuffed, he went to the bar, ordered doubles, and returned to her side. He was ruddy-featured, and one size larger than his dark blue suit. Only his eyes betrayed any sign of nervousness, resting on her for moments only, then darting away like startled fish.

There would be no serious conversation: that she had already decided. She didn't want to know much about him. His name, if necessary. His profession and marital status, if he insisted. Beyond that let him be just a body.

As it was there was no danger of a confessional. She'd met more talkative paving stones. He smiled occasionally, a short, nervous smile that showed teeth too even to be real – and offered further drinks. She said no, wanting the chase over with as soon as possible, and instead asked if he had time for a coffee. He said he had.

'The house is only a few minutes from here,' she replied, and they went to her car. She kept wondering, as she drove – the meat on the seat beside her – why this was so very easy. Was it that the man was plainly a victim – with his ineffectual eyes and his artificial teeth – born, did he but know it, to make this journey? Yes; perhaps that was it. She was not afraid because all of this was so perfectly predictable . . .

As she turned the key in the front door, and stepped into the house, she thought she heard a noise in the kitchen. Had Rory returned home early: ill perhaps? She called out. There was no reply; the house was empty. Almost.

From the threshold on, she had the thing planned meticulously. She closed the door. The man in the blue suit stared at his manicured hands, and waited for his cue.

'I get lonely sometimes,' she told him, as she brushed past him. It was a line she'd come up with in bed the previous night.

He only nodded by way of response, the expression on his face a mingling of fear and incredulity; he clearly couldn't quite believe his luck.

'Do you want another drink?' she asked him. 'Or shall we go straight upstairs?'

He nodded again. 'I think maybe I've drunk enough already.'

'Upstairs then.'

He made an indecisive move in her direction, as though he might have intended a kiss. She wanted no courtship, however. Skirting his touch, she crossed to the bottom of the stairs.

'I'll lead,' she said. Meekly, he followed.

At the top of the steps she glanced around at him, and caught him dabbing sweat from his chin with his handkerchief. She waited until he caught up with her, and then led him halfway along the landing to the damp room.

The door had been left ajar.

'Come on in,' she said.

He obeyed. Once inside it took him a few moments to become accustomed to the gloom, and a further time to give voice to his observation that: 'There's no bed.'

She closed the door, and switched on the light. She had hung one of Rory's old jackets on the back of the door. In its pocket she'd left the knife.

He said again: '. . . no bed.'

'What's wrong with the floor?' she replied.

'The floor?'

'Take off your jacket. You're warm.'

'I am,' he agreed, but did nothing, so she moved across to him, and began to slip the knot of his tie. He was trembling, poor lamb. Poor, bleatless lamb. While she removed the tie, he began to shrug off his jacket.

Was Frank watching this, she wondered? Her eyes strayed momentarily to the wall. Yes, she thought; he's there. He *sees*. He *knows*. He licks his lips and grows impatient.

The lamb spoke. 'Why don't you . . .' he began, 'why don't you maybe . . . do the same?'

'Would you like to see me naked?' she teased. The words made his eyes gleam.

'Yes,' he said quickly. 'Yes. I'd like that.'

'Very much?'

'Very much.'

He was unbuttoning his shirt.

'Maybe you will,' she said.

He gave her the dwarf smile again.

'Is it a game?' he ventured.

'If you want it to be,' she said, and helped him out of his shirt. His body was pale and waxy, like a fungus. His upper chest heavy; his belly too. She put her hands to his face. He kissed her fingertips.

'You're beautiful,' he said, spitting the words out as though they'd been vexing him for hours.

'Am I?'

'You know you are. Lovely. Loveliest woman I ever set eyes on.'

'That's gallant of you,' she said, and turned back to the door. Behind her she heard his belt buckle clink, and the sound of cloth slipping over skin as he dropped his trousers.

So far and no further, she thought. She had no wish to see him babe-naked. It was enough to have him like this –

She reached into the jacket pocket.

'Oh dear,' the lamb suddenly said.

She let the knife lie. 'What is it?' she asked, turning to look at him. If the ring on his finger hadn't already given his status away, she would have known him to be a married man by the underpants he wore: baggy and overwashed, an unflattering garment bought by a wife who had long since ceased to think of her husband in sexual terms.

'I think I need to empty my bladder,' he said. 'Too many whiskies.'

She shrugged a small shrug, and turned back to the door.

'Won't be a moment,' he said at her back. But her hand was in the jacket pocket before the words were out, and as he stepped towards the door she turned on him, slaughtering knife in hand.

His pace was too quick to see the blade until the very last moment, and even then it was bemusement that crossed his face, not fear. It was a short-lived look. The knife was in him in a moment after, slicing his belly with the ease of a blade in over-ripe cheese. She opened one cut, and then another.

As the blood started, she was certain the room flickered, the bricks and mortar trembling to see the spurts that flew from him.

She had a breath's length to admire the phenomena, no more, before the lamb let out a wheezing curse, and — instead of moving out of the knife's range as she had anticipated — took a step towards her and knocked the weapon from her hand. It spun across the floorboards and collided with the skirting. Then he was upon her.

He put his hand into her hair, and took a fistful. It seemed his intention was not violence but escape, for he relinquished his hold as soon as he'd pulled her away from the door. She fell against the wall, looking up to see him wrestling with the door-handle, his free hand clamped to his cuts.

She was quick now. Across to where the knife lay, up, and back towards him in one fluid motion. He had got the door open by inches, but not far enough. She brought the knife down in the middle of his pock-marked back. He yelled, and released the door-handle. She was already drawing the knife out, and plunging into him a second time, and now a third and fourth. Indeed she lost count of the wounds she made, her attack lent venom by his refusal to lie down and die. He stumbled around the room, grieving and complaining, blood flowing on to his buttocks and legs. Finally, after an age of this farcical stuff, he keeled over and hit the floor.

This time she was certain her senses did not deceive her. The room, or the spirit in it, responded with soft sighs of anticipation.

Somewhere a bell was ringing . . .

Almost as an afterthought, she registered that the lamb had stopped breathing. She crossed the blood-spattered floor to where he lay, and said: 'Enough?'

Then she went to wash her face.

As she moved down the landing she heard the room groan – there was no other word for it. She stopped in her tracks, almost tempted to go back. But the blood was drying on her hands, and its stickiness revolted her.

In the bathroom she stripped off her flower-patterned blouse, and rinsed first her hands, then her speckled arms, and finally her neck. The dousing both chilled and braced her. It felt good. That done, she washed the knife, rinsed the sink, and returned along the landing without bothering to dry herself or to dress.

She had no need for either. The room was like a furnace, as the dead man's energies pulsed from his body. They didn't get far. Already the blood on the floor was crawling away towards the wall where Frank was, the beads seeming to boil and evaporate as they came within sight of the skirting board. She watched, entranced. But there was more. Something was happening to the corpse. It was being drained of every nutritious element, the body convulsing as its innards were sucked out; gases moaning in its bowels and throat, the skin desiccating in front of her startled eyes. At one point the plastic teeth dropped back into the gullet, and the gums withered around them.

And in mere moments, it was done. Anything the body might have usefully offered by way of nourishment had been taken; the husk that remained would not have sustained a family of fleas. She was impressed.

Suddenly, the bulb began to flicker. She looked to the wall, expecting it to tremble and spit her love from hiding. But no. The bulb went out. There was only the dim light that crept through the age-beaten blind.

'Where are you?' she said.

The walls remained mute.

'Where are you?'

Still nothing. The room was cooling. Her breasts had grown gooseflesh. She peered down at the luminous watch on the lamb's shrivelled arm. It ticked away, indifferent to the apocalypse that had overtaken its owner. It read four forty-one. Rory would be back anytime after five-fifteen, depending on how dense the traffic was. She had work to do before then.

Bundling up the blue suit and the rest of his clothes, she put them in several plastic bags, and then went in search of a larger bag for the remains. She had expected Frank to be here to help her with this labour, but as he hadn't shown she had no choice but to do it herself. When she came back to the room, the deterioration of the lamb was still continuing, though now much slowed. Perhaps Frank was still finding nutrients to squeeze from the corpse, but she doubted it. More likely the pauperized body, sucked clean of marrow and every vital fluid, was no longer strong enough to support itself. When she had parcelled it up in the bag, it was the weight of a small child, no more. Sealing the bag up, she was about to take it down to the car when she heard the front door open.

The sound undammed all the panic she'd so assiduously kept from herself. She began to shake. Tears pricked her sinuses.

'*Not now . . .*' she told herself, but the feeling would simply not be suppressed any longer.

In the hallway below, Rory said: 'Sweetheart?'

Sweetheart! She could have laughed, but for the terror. She was here if he wanted to find her – his sweetheart, his honeybun – with her breasts new-washed, and a dead man in her arms.

'Where are you?'

She hesitated before replying, not certain that her larynx was the equal of the deception.

He called a third time, his voice changing timbre as he walked through into the kitchen. It would take him a moment only to discover that she wasn't at the cooker stirring sauce; then he would come back and head up the stairs. She had ten seconds; fifteen at most.

Attempting to keep her tread as light as possible, for fear he heard her movements overhead, she carried the bundle to the spare room at the end of the landing. Too small to be used as a bedroom (except perhaps for a child), they had used it as a dump. Half-emptied tea chests; pieces of furniture they had not found a place for; all manner of rubbish. Here she laid the body to rest awhile, behind an upended armchair. Then she locked the door behind her, just as Rory called from the bottom of the stairs. He was coming up.

'Julia? Julia, sweetheart. Are you there?'

61

She slipped into the bathroom, and consulted the mirror. It showed her a flushed portrait. She picked up the blouse she'd left hanging over the side of the bath, and put it on. It smelt stale, and there was undoubtedly blood spattered between the flowers, but she had nothing else to wear.

He was coming along the landing; she heard his elephantine tread.

'Julia?'

This time she answered – making no attempt to disguise the tremulous quality of her voice. The mirror had confirmed what she feared: that there was no way she could pass herself off as undistressed. She was obliged to make a virtue of the liability.

'Are you all right?' he asked her. He was outside the door.

'No,' she said. 'I'm feeling sick.'

'Oh, darling . . .'

'I'll be fine in a minute.'

He tried the handle, but she'd bolted the door.

'Can you leave me alone for a little while?'

'Do you want a doctor?'

'No,' she told him. 'No. Really. But I wouldn't mind a brandy – '

'Brandy . . .'

'I'll be down in two ticks.'

'Whatever madam wants,' he quipped. She counted his steps as he trudged to the stairs, then descended. Once she'd calculated that he was out of earshot, she slid back the bolt and stepped on to the landing.

The late afternoon light was failing quickly; the landing was a murky tunnel.

Downstairs, she heard the clink of glass on glass. She moved as quickly as she dared to Frank's room.

There was no sound from the gloomed interior. The walls no longer trembled; nor did distant bells toll. She pushed the door open; it creaked slightly.

She had not entirely tidied up after her labours. There was dust on the floor, human dust; and fragments of dried flesh. She went down on her haunches and collected them up diligently. Rory had been right. What a perfect *hausfrau* she made.

As she stood up again, something shifted in the ever-denser shadows of the room. She looked in the direction of the movement but before her eyes could make sense of the form in the corner, a voice said: 'Don't look at me.'

It was a tired voice – the voice of somebody used up by events; but it was *concrete*. The syllables were carried on the same air that she breathed.

'Frank,' she said.

'Yes . . .' came the broken voice, '. . . it's me.'

From downstairs, Rory called up to her. 'Are you feeling better?'

She went to the door.

'Much better . . .' she responded. At her back the hidden thing said: '*Don't let him near me,*' the words coming fast and fierce.

'It's all right,' she whispered to him. Then, to Rory: 'I'll be with you in a minute. Put on some music. Something soothing.'

Rory replied that he would, and retired to the lounge.

'I'm only half-made,' Frank's voice said. 'I don't want you to see me . . . don't want *anybody* to see

63

me . . . not like this . . .' The words were halting once more, and wretched. 'I have to have more blood, Julia.'

'More?'

'And soon.'

'How much more?' she asked the shadows. This time she caught a better glimpse of what lay in wait there. No wonder he wanted no-one to look.

'Just *more*,' he said. Though the volume was barely above a whisper, there was an urgency in the voice that made her afraid.

'I have to go . . .' she said, hearing music from below.

This time the darkness made no reply. At the door, she turned back.

'I'm glad you came,' she said. As she closed the door she heard a sound not unlike laughter behind her; nor unlike sobs.

SEVEN

'Kirsty? Is that you?'
        'Yes? Who is this?'
'It's Rory . . .'
The line was watery; as though the deluge outside had seeped down the phone. Still, she was happy to hear from him. He called up so seldom, and when he did it was usually on behalf of both himself and Julia. Not this time, however. This time Julia was the subject under discussion.

'There's something wrong with her, Kirsty,' he said. 'I don't know what.'

'Ill, you mean?'

'Maybe. She's just so strange with me. And she looks terrible.'

'Have you said anything to her?'

'She says she's fine. But she isn't; I wondered if maybe she'd spoken with you.'

'I haven't set eyes on her since your house-warming.'

'That's another thing. She doesn't even want to leave the house. That's not like her.'

'Do you want me to . . . to have a word with her?'

'Would you?'

'I don't know if it'll do any good, but I'll try.'

'Don't say anything about me talking to you.'

'Of course not. I'll call in at the house tomorrow – '

('*Tomorrow. It has to be tomorrow.*'

'*Yes . . . I know.*'

'*I'm afraid I'll lose my grip, Julia. Start slipping back.*')

'I'll give you a call from the office on Thursday. You can tell me what you make of her.'

('*Slipping back?*'

'*They'll know I've gone by now.*'

'*Who will?*'

'*The Gash. The bastards that took me . . .*'

'*They're waiting for you?*'

'*Just beyond the wall.*')

Rory told her how grateful he was, and she in turn told him that it was the least a friend could do. Then he put down the phone, leaving her listening to the rain on the empty line.

Now they were both Julia's creatures, looking after her welfare, fretting for her if she had bad dreams.

No matter, it was a kind of togetherness.

2

The man with the white tie had not bided his time. Almost as soon as he set eyes on Julia he came across to her. She decided, even as he approached, that he was not suitable. Too big; too confident. After the way the first one had fought, she was determined to

66

choose with care. So, when White Tie asked what she was drinking, she told him to leave her be.

He was apparently used to rejections, and took it in his stride, withdrawing to the bar. She returned to her drink.

It was raining heavily today – had been raining now for seventy-two hours, on and off – and there were fewer customers than there had been the week before. One or two drowned rats headed in from the street, but none looked her way for more than a few moments. And time was moving on. It was already past two. She wasn't going to risk getting caught again by Rory's return. She emptied her glass, and decided that this was not Frank's lucky day. Then she stepped out of the bar into the downpour, put up her umbrella, and headed back to the car. As she went she heard footsteps behind her, and then White Tie was at her side and saying: 'My hotel's nearby.'

'Oh . . .' she said, and kept on walking. But he wasn't going to be shrugged off so easily.

'I'm only here for two days,' he said.

Don't tempt me, she thought.

'Just looking for some companionship . . .' he went on. 'I haven't spoken to a soul.'

'Is that right?'

He took hold of her wrist. A grip so tight she almost cried out. That was when she knew she was going to have to kill him. He seemed to see the desire in her eyes.

'My hotel?' he said.

'I don't much like hotels. They're so impersonal.'

'Have you got a better idea?' he said to her.

She had, of course.

He hung his dripping raincoat on the hall stand and she offered him a drink, which he welcomed. His name was Patrick, and he was from Newcastle.

'Down on business. Can't seem to get much done.'

'Why's that?'

He shrugged. 'I'm probably a bad salesman. Simple as that.'

'What do you sell?' she asked him.

'What do you care?' he replied, razor quick.

She grinned. She would have to get him upstairs quickly, before she started to enjoy his company.

'Why don't we dispense with the small talk?' she said. It was a stale line, but it was the first thing that came to her tongue. He swallowed the last of his drink in one gulp, and went where she led.

This time she had not left the door ajar. It was locked, which plainly intrigued him.

'After you,' he said, when the door swung open.

She went first. He followed. This time, she had decided, there would be no stripping. If some nourishment was soaked up by his clothes then so be it, she was not going to give him a chance to realize that they weren't alone in the room.

'Going to fuck on the floor are we?' he asked casually.

'Any objections?'

'Not if it suits you,' he said and clamped his mouth over hers, his tongue frisking her teeth for cavities. There was some passion in him, she mused; she could feel him hard against her already. But she had work to do here: blood to spill and a mouth to feed.

She broke his kiss, and tried to slip from his arms.

68

The knife was back in the jacket on the door. While it was out of reach she had little power to resist him.

'What's the problem?' he said.

'No problem . . .' she murmured. 'There's no hurry either. We've got all the time in the world.' She touched the front of his trousers, to reassure him. Like a stroked dog, he closed his eyes.

'You're a strange one . . .' he said.

'Don't look,' she told him.

'Huh?'

'Keep your eyes closed.'

He frowned, but obeyed. She took a step backwards towards the door, and half-turned to fumble in the depths of the pocket, glancing back to see that he was still blind.

He was; and unzipping himself. As her hand clasped the knife, the shadows growled.

He heard the noise. His eyes sprang open.

'What was that?' he said, reeling around and peering into the darkness.

'It was nothing,' she insisted, as she pulled the knife from its hiding place. He was moving away from her, across the room.

'There's somebody — '

'*Don't.*'

'— here.'

The last syllable faltered on his lips, as he glimpsed a fretful motion in the corner beside the window.

'What . . . in God's . . . ?' he began. As he pointed into the darkness she was at him, and slicing his neck open with a butcher's efficiency. Blood jumped immediately, a fat spurt that hit the wall with a wet thud. She heard Frank's pleasure, and then the dying

69

man's complaint; long and low. His hand went up to his neck to stem the pulse, but she was at him again, slicing his pleading hand, his face. He staggered, he sobbed. Finally, he collapsed, twitching.

She stepped away from him to avoid the flailing legs. In the corner of the room she saw Frank rocking to and fro.

'Good woman . . .' he said.

Was it her imagination, or was his voice already stronger than it had been? More like the voice she'd heard in her head a thousand times these plundered years?

The door-bell rang. She froze.

'Oh Jesus,' her mouth said.

'It's all right . . .' the shadow replied. 'He's as good as dead.'

She looked at the man in the white tie, and saw that Frank was right. The twitching had all but ceased.

'He's big,' said Frank. 'And healthy.'

He was moving into her sight, too greedy for sustenance to prohibit her stare; she saw him plainly now for the first time. He was a travesty. Not just of humanity, of life. She looked away.

The door-bell was ringing again, and for longer.

'Go and answer it,' Frank asked her.

She made no reply.

'*Go on,*' he told her, turning his foul head in her direction, his eyes keen and bright in the surrounding corruption.

The bell rang a third time.

'Your caller is very insistent,' he said, trying persuasion where demands had failed, 'I really think you should answer the door.'

She backed away from him, and he turned his attentions back to the body on the floor.

Again, the bell.

It was better to answer it perhaps (she was already out of the room, trying not to hear the sounds Frank was making) – better to open the door to the day. It would be a man selling insurance, most likely, or a Jehovah's Witness, with news of salvation. Yes; she wouldn't mind hearing that. The bell rang again. 'Coming,' she said, hurrying now for fear he'd leave. She had welcome on her face when she opened the door. It died immediately.

'Kirsty.'

'I was just about to give up on you.'

'I was . . . I was asleep.'

'Oh.'

Kirsty looked at the apparition that had opened the door to her. From Rory's description she'd expected a washed-out creature. What she saw was quite the reverse. Julia's face was flushed; strands of sweat-darkened hair glued to her brow. She did not look like a woman who had just risen from sleep. A bed, perhaps; but not sleep.

'I just called by – ' Kirsty said, ' – for a chat.'

Julia made a half-shrug.

'Well, it's not convenient just at the moment,' she said.

'I see.'

'Maybe we could speak later in the week . . . ?'

Kirsty's gaze drifted past Julia to the coat stand in the hall. A man's gaberdine hung from one of the pegs, still damp.

'Is Rory in?' she ventured.

'No,' Julia said. 'Of course not. He's at work.' Her face hardened. 'Is that what you came round for?' she said, 'to see Rory?'

'No, I – '

'You don't have to ask my permission, you know. He's a grown man. You two can do what the fuck you like.'

Kirsty didn't try to debate the point. The *volte face* left her dizzied.

'Go home,' Julia said. 'I don't want to talk to you.'

She slammed the door.

Kirsty stood on the step for half a minute, shaking. She had little doubt of what was going on. The dripping raincoat; Julia's agitation – her flushed face, her sudden anger. She had a lover in the house. Poor Rory had misread all the signs.

She deserted the doorstep, and started down the path to the street. A crowd of thoughts jostled for her attention. At last, one came clear of the pack: how would she tell Rory? His heart would break, she had no doubt of that. And she, the luckless tale-teller, she would be tainted with the news, wouldn't she? She felt tears close.

They didn't come, however; another sensation, more insistent, overtook them as she stepped on to the pavement from the path.

She was being watched. She could feel the look at the back of her head. Was it Julia? Somehow, she thought not. The lover then. Yes, the lover!

Safely out of the shadow of the house, she succumbed to the urge to turn and look.

In the damp room, Frank stared through the hole he had made in the blind. The visitor – whose face he vaguely recognized – was staring up at the house; at his very window, indeed. Confident that she would see nothing of him, he stared back. He had certainly set his eyes on more voluptuous creatures, but something about her lack of glamour engaged him. Such women were in his experience often more entertaining company than beauties like Julia. They could be flattered or bullied into acts the beauties would never countenance; and be grateful for the attention. Perhaps she would come back, this woman. He hoped she would.

Kirsty scanned the facade of the house, but it was blank; the windows were either empty or curtained. Yet the feeling of her being watched persisted; indeed it was so strong she turned away in embarrassment.

The rain started again as she walked along Lodovico Street, and she welcomed it. It cooled her blushes, and gave cover to tears that would be postponed no longer.

3

Julia had gone back upstairs trembling, and found White Tie at the door. Or rather, his head. This time, either out of an excess of greed or malice, Frank had dismembered the corpse. Pieces of bone and dried meat lay scattered about the room.

There was no sign of the gourmet himself.

She turned back towards the door, and he was there, blocking her path. Mere minutes had passed

73

since she'd seen him bending to drain energy from the dead man. In that brief time he had changed out of all recognition. Where there had been withered cartilage there was now ripening muscle; the map of his arteries and veins was being drawn anew: they pulsed with stolen life. There was even a sprouting of hair, somewhat premature perhaps given his absence of skin, on the raw ball of his head.

None of this sweetened his appearance a jot. Indeed in many ways it worsened it. Previously there had been scarcely anything recognizable about him, but now there were scraps of humanity everywhere, throwing into yet greater relief the catastrophic nature of his wounding.

There was worse to come. He spoke, and when he spoke it was with a voice that was indisputably Frank's. The broken syllables had gone.

'I feel pain,' he said.

His browless, half-lidded eyes were watching her every response. She tried to conceal the queasiness she felt, but knew the disguise inadequate.

'My nerves are working again . . .' he was telling her, '. . . and they *hurt*.'

'What can I do about it?' she asked him.

'Maybe . . . maybe some bandages.'

'Bandages?'

'Help me bind myself together.'

'If that's what you want.'

'But I need more than that, Julia. I need another body.'

'Another?' she said. Was there no end to this?

'What's to lose?' he replied, moving closer to her.

At his sudden proximity she became very anxious. Reading the fear in her face, he stopped his advance.

'I'll be whole soon . . .' he promised her, 'and when I am . . .'

'I'd better clean up,' she said, averting her gaze from him.

'When I am, sweet Julia . . .'

'Rory will be home soon.'

'*Rory!*' He spat the name out. 'My darling brother! How in God's name did you come to marry such a dullard?'

She felt a spasm of anger towards Frank. 'I love him,' she said. And then after a moment's pondering, corrected herself. 'I thought I loved him.'

His laugh only made his dreadful nakedness more apparent. 'How can you believe that?' he said. 'He's a slug. Always was. Always will be. Never had any sense of adventure.'

'Unlike you.'

'Unlike me.'

She looked down at the floor. A dead man's hand lay between them. For an instant she was almost overwhelmed by self-revulsion. All that she had done, and dreamt of doing, in the last few days rose up in front of her: a parade of seductions that had ended in death – all for this death that she had hoped so fervently would end in seduction. She was as damned as he, she thought; no fouler ambition could nest in his head than the one that presently cooed and fluttered in hers.

Well . . . it was done.

'Heal me,' he whispered to her. The harshness had

gone from his voice. He spoke like a lover. 'Heal me . . . please.'

'I will,' she said. 'I promise you I will.'

'And then we'll be together.'

She frowned.

'What about Rory?'

'We're brothers under the skin,' Frank said. 'I'll make him see the wisdom of this; the miracle of it. You don't belong to him, Julia. Not any more.'

'No,' she said. It was true.

'We belong to each other. That's what you want isn't it?'

'It's what I want.'

'You know I think if I'd had you I wouldn't have despaired,' he said to her. 'Wouldn't have given away my body and soul so cheaply.'

'Cheaply?'

'For pleasure. For mere sensuality. In you . . .' – here he moved towards her again. This time his words held her; she didn't retreat – '. . . in you I might have discovered some reason to live.'

'I'm here,' she said. Without thinking, she reached across and touched him. The body was hot, and damp. His pulse seemed to be everywhere. In every tender bud of nerve; in each burgeoning sinew. The contact excited her. It was as if, until this moment, she had never quite believed him to be real. Now it was incontestable. She had *made* this man, or re-made him; used her wit and her cunning to give him substance. The thrill she felt, touching this too vulnerable body, was the thrill of ownership.

'This is the most dangerous time,' he told her.

'Before now I could hide myself. I was practically nothing at all. But not any more.'

'No. I've thought of that.'

'We must be done with it quickly. I must be strong and whole; at whatever cost. You agree?'

'Of course.'

'After that there'll be an end to the waiting, Julia.'

The pulse in him seemed to quicken at the thought.

Then he was kneeling in front of her. His unfinished hands were at her hips; then his mouth.

Forsaking the dregs of her distaste, she put her hand upon his head, and felt the hair – silken, like a baby's – and the shell of his skull beneath. He had learned nothing of delicacy since last he'd held her. But despair had taught her the fine art of squeezing blood from stones; with time she would have love from this hateful thing, or know the reason why.

EIGHT

There was thunder that night. A storm without rain, which made the air smell of steel.

Kirsty had never slept well. Even as a child, though her mother had known lullabies enough to pacify nations, the girl had never found slumber easy. It wasn't that she had bad dreams: or at least none that lingered until morning. It was that sleep itself – the act of closing the eyes and relinquishing control of her consciousness – was something she was temperamentally unsuited to.

Tonight, with the thunder so loud and the lightning so bright, she was happy. She had an excuse to forsake her tangled bed, and drink tea, and watch the spectacle from her window.

It gave her time to think, as well; time to turn over the problem which had vexed her since leaving the house in Lodovico Street. But she was still no nearer an answer.

One particular doubt nagged. Suppose she was wrong about what she'd seen? Suppose she'd misconstrued the evidence, and Julia had a perfectly good explanation? She would lose Rory at a stroke.

And yet, how could she remain silent? She couldn't bear to think of the woman laughing behind her back, exploiting his gentility, his naïveté. The thought made her blood boil.

The only other option was to wait and watch; to see if she could gain some incontrovertible evidence. If her worst suppositions were then confirmed, she would have no choice but to tell Rory all she'd seen.

Yes. That was the answer. Wait and watch; watch and wait.

The thunder rolled around for long hours, denying her sleep until nearly four. When, finally, she did sleep, it was the slumber of a watcher and waiter. Light, and full of sighs.

2

The storm made a ghost-train of the house. Julia sat downstairs and counted the beats between the flash and the fury that came on its heels. She had never liked thunder. She, a murderess; she, a consorter with the living dead. It was another paradox to add to the thousands she'd found at work in herself of late. She thought more than once of going upstairs, and taking some comfort with the prodigy; but knew that it would be unwise. Rory might return at any moment from his office party. He would be drunk, on past experience, and full of unwelcome fondness.

The storm crept closer. She put on the television, to block out the din, which it scarcely did.

At eleven, Rory came home, wreathed in smiles. He had good news. In the middle of the party his supervisor had taken him aside, commended him for his excellent work, and spoken of great things for the future. Julia listened to his retelling of the exchange, hoping that his inebriation would blind him to her indifference. At last, his news told, he threw off his jacket and sat down on the sofa beside her.

'Poor you,' he said. 'You don't like the thunder.'

'I'm fine,' she said.

'Are you sure?'

'Yes. Fine.'

He leaned across to her, and nuzzled her ear.

'You're sweaty,' she said matter-of-factly. He didn't cease his overtures, however, unwilling to lower his baton now he'd begun.

'*Please*, Rory —' she said. 'I don't want this.'

'Why not? What did I do?'

'Nothing,' she said, pretending some interest in the television. 'You're fine.'

'Oh is that right?' he said. '*You're* fine. *I'm* fine. Everybody's fucking fine.'

She stared at the flickering screen. The late evening news had just begun; the usual crop of sorrows full to brimming. Rory talked on, drowning out the newscaster's voice with his diatribe. She didn't mind much. What did the world have to tell her? Little enough. Whereas she, *she* had news for the world that it would reel to hear. About the condition of the damned; about love lost, and then found; about what despair and desire have in common.

'Please, Julia —' Rory was saying, ' — just speak to me . . .'

The pleas demanded her attention. He looked, she thought, like the boy in the photographs — his body

81

hirsute and bloated, his clothes those of an adult, but still, in essence, a boy, with his bewildered gaze and sulky mouth. She remembered Frank's question: *'How could you ever marry such a dullard?'* Thinking of it, a sour smile creased her lips. He looked at her, his puzzlement deepening.

'What's so funny, damn you?'

'Nothing.'

He shook his head, dull anger replacing the sulk. A peal of thunder followed the lightning with barely a beat intervening. As it came, there was a noise from the floor above. She turned her attention back to the television to divert Rory's interest. But it was a vain attempt; he'd heard the sound.

'What the fuck was that?'

'Thunder.'

He stood up. 'No,' he said. 'Something else.' He was already at the door.

A dozen options raced through her head, none of them practical. He wrestled drunkenly with the door-handle.

'Maybe I left a window open,' she said, and got up. 'I'll go and see.'

'I can do it,' he replied. 'I'm not totally inept.'

'Nobody said – ' she began, but he wasn't listening. As he stepped out into the hallway the lightning came with the thunder: loud and bright. As she went in pursuit of him another flash came fast upon the first, accompanied by a bowel-rocking crash. Rory was already halfway up the stairs.

'It was nothing!' she shouted after him. He made no reply, but climbed on to the top of the stairs. She followed.

'Don't . . .' she said to him, in a lull between one peal and the next. When she reached the top of the stairs he was waiting.

'Something wrong?' he said.

She hid her trepidation behind a shrug. 'You're being silly,' she replied softly.

'Am I?'

'It was just the thunder.'

His face, lit from the hall below, suddenly softened. 'Why do you treat me like shit?' he asked her.

'You're just tired,' she told him.

'Why though?' he persisted, child-like. 'What have I ever done to you?'

'It's all right,' she said. 'Really, Rory. Everything's all right.' The same hypnotic banalities, over and over.

Again, the thunder. And beneath the din, another sound. She cursed Frank's indiscretion.

Rory turned, and looked along the darkened landing.

'Hear that?' he asked.

'No.'

His limbs dogged by drink, he moved away from her. She watched him recede into shadow. Lightning, spilling through the open bedroom door, flash-lit him; then darkness again. He was walking towards the damp room. Towards Frank.

'Wait . . .' she said, and went after him.

He didn't halt, but covered the few yards to the door. As she reached him his hand was closing on the handle.

Inspired by panic, she reached out and touched his cheek. 'I'm afraid . . .' she said.

He looked round at her woozily.

'What of?' he asked her.

She moved her hand to his lips, letting him taste the fear on her fingers.

'The storm,' she said.

She could see the wetness of his eyes in the gloom; little more. Was he swallowing the hook, or spitting it out?

Then: 'Poor baby,' he said.

Swallowed, she elated; and reaching down she put her hand over his and drew it from the door. If Frank so much as breathed now, all was lost.

'Poor baby,' he said again, and wrapped an embrace around her. His balance was not too good; he was a lead weight in her arms.

'Come on,' she said, coaxing him away from the door. He went with her for a couple of stumbling paces, and then lost his equilibrium. She let go of him, and reached out to the wall for support. The lightning came again, and by it she saw that his eyes had found her, and glittered.

'I love you,' he said, stepping across the hallway to where she stood. He pressed against her, so heavily there was no resisting. His head went to the crook of her neck, muttering sweet-talk into her skin; now he was kissing her. She wanted to throw him off. More, she wanted to take him by his clammy hand and show him the death-defying monster he had been so close to stumbling across.

But Frank wasn't ready for that confrontation; not yet. All she could do was endure Rory's caresses and hope that exhaustion claimed him quickly.

'Why don't we go downstairs?' she suggested.

He muttered something into her neck; and didn't move. His left hand was on her breast, the other clasped around her waist. She let him work his fingers beneath her blouse. To resist at this juncture would only inflame him afresh.

'I need you,' he said, raising his mouth to her ear. Once, half a lifetime ago, her heart had seemed to skip at such a profession. Now she knew better. Her heart was no acrobat; there was no tingle in the coils of her abdomen. Only the steady workings of her body. Breath drawn, blood circulated, food pulped and purged. Thinking of her anatomy thus, untainted by romanticism – as a collection of natural imperatives housed in muscle and bone – she found it easier to let him strip her blouse, and put his face to her breasts. Her nerve-endings dutifully responded to his tongue; but again, it was merely an anatomy lesson. She stood back in the dome of her skull, and was unmoved.

He was unbuttoning himself now; she caught sight of the boastful plum as he stroked it against her thigh. Now he opened her legs, and pulled her underwear down just far enough to give him access. She made no objection, nor even a sound, as he made his entrance.

His own din began almost immediately, feeble claims of love and lust hopelessly tangled together. She half-listened, and let him work at his play, his face buried in her hair.

Closing her eyes, she tried to picture better times, but the lightning spoilt her dreaming. As sound followed light, she opened her eyes again to see that the door of the damp room had been opened two or three inches. In the narrow gap between door and frame she could just make out a glistening figure, watching them.

She could not see Frank's eyes, but she felt them sharpened beyond pricking by envy and rage. Nor did she look away, but stared on at the shadow while Rory's moans increased. And at the end one moment became another, and she was lying on the bed with her wedding dress crushed beneath her, while a black and scarlet beast crept up between her legs to give her a sample of its love.

'Poor baby,' was the last thing Rory said as sleep overcame him. He lay on the bed still dressed; she made no attempt to strip him. When his snores were even, she left him to it, and went back to the room.

Frank was standing beside the window, watching the storm move to the south-east. He had torn the blind away. Lamplight washed the walls.

'He heard you,' she said.

'I had to see the storm,' he replied simply. 'I needed it.'

'He almost found you, damn it.'

Frank shook his head. 'There's no such thing as almost,' he said, still staring out of the window. Then, after a pause: 'I want to be out there. I want to *have* it all again.'

'I know.'

'No you don't,' he told her. 'You've no conception of the hunger I've got on me.'

'Tomorrow then,' she said. 'I'll get another body tomorrow.'

'Yes. You do that. And I want some other stuff. A radio for one. I want to know what's going on out there. And food: proper food. Fresh bread – '

'Whatever you need.'

' – and ginger. The preserved kind, you know? In syrup.'

'I know.'

He glanced round at her briefly, but he wasn't seeing her. There was too much world to be reacquainted with tonight.

'I didn't realize it was autumn,' he said, and went back to watching the storm.

NINE

The first thing Kirsty noticed when she came round the corner of Lodovico Street the following day, was that the blind had gone from the upper front window. Sheets of newspaper had been taped against the glass in its place.

She found herself a vantage point in the shelter of a holly hedge, from which she could hopefully watch the house but remain unseen. Then she settled down for her vigil.

It was not quickly rewarded. Two hours and more went by before she saw Julia leave the house, another hour and a quarter before she returned; by which time Kirsty's feet were numb with cold.

Julia had not returned alone. The man she was with was not known to Kirsty; nor indeed did he look to be a likely member of Julia's circle. From a distance he appeared to be in middle-age: stocky; balding. When he followed Julia into the house he gave a nervous backwards glance, as if fearful of voyeurs.

She waited in her hiding place for a further quarter of an hour, not certain of what to do next. Did she linger here until the man emerged, and challenge him? Or did she go to the house and try to talk her way inside? Neither option was particularly attractive. She decided not to decide. Instead she would get closer to the house, and see what inspiration the moment brought.

The answer was: very little. As she made her way up the path her feet itched to turn and carry her away. Indeed she was within an ace of doing just that when she heard a shout from within.

The man's name was Sykes; Stanley Sykes. Nor was that all he'd told Julia on the way back from the bar. She knew his wife's name (Maudie) and occupation (assistant chiropodist); she'd had pictures of the children (Rebecca and Ethan) provided for her to coo over. The man seemed to be defying her to continue the seduction. She merely smiled, and told him he was a lucky man.

But once in the house, things had begun to go awry. Halfway up the stairs friend Sykes had suddenly announced that what they were doing was *wrong* – that God saw them, and knew their hearts, and found them wanting. She had done her best to calm him, but he was not to be won back from the Lord. Instead, he lost his temper and flailed out at her. He might have done worse, in his righteous wrath, but for the voice that had called him from the landing. He'd stopped hitting her instantly, and become so pale it was as if he believed God himself was doing the calling. Then Frank had appeared at the top of the stairs, in all his glory. Sykes had loosed a cry, and tried to run. But Julia was quick. She had her hand on him long enough for Frank to descend the few stairs and make a permanent arrest.

She had not realized, until she heard the creak and snap of bone as Frank took hold of his prey, how strong he had become of late: stronger surely than a natural man. At Frank's touch Sykes had shouted again. To silence him, Frank had wrenched off his jaw.

The second shout that Kirsty heard had ended abruptly, but she read enough panic in the din to have her at the door, and on the verge of knocking.

Only then did she think better of it. Instead, she slipped down the side of the house, doubting with every step the wisdom of this, but equally certain that a frontal assault would get her nowhere. The gate that offered access to the back garden was lacking a bolt. She slipped through, her ears alive to every sound, especially that of her own feet. From the house, nothing. Not so much as a moan.

Leaving the gate open in case she should need a quick retreat, she hurried to the back door. It was unlocked. This time, she let doubt slow her step. Maybe she should go and call Rory; bring him to the house. But by that time whatever was happening inside would be over, and she knew damn well that unless Julia was caught red-handed she would slide from under any accusation. No; this was the only way. She stepped inside.

The house remained completely quiet. There was not even a footfall to help her locate the actors she'd come to view. She moved to the kitchen door, and from there through to the dining room. Her stomach twitched; her throat was suddenly so dry she could barely swallow.

From dining room to lounge, and thence into the hallway. Still nothing; whisper or sigh. Julia and her companion could only be upstairs, which suggested that she had been wrong, thinking she heard fear in the shouts. Perhaps it was pleasure that she'd heard. An orgasmic whoop, instead of the terror she'd taken it for. It was an easy mistake to make.

The front door was on her right, mere yards away. She could still slip out and away, the coward in her tempted, and no-one be any the wiser. But a fierce curiosity had seized her, a desire to know (to *see*) the mysteries the house held, and be done with them. As she climbed the stairs the curiosity mounted to a kind of exhilaration.

She reached the top, and began to make her way along the landing. The thought occurred now that the birds had flown; that while she had been creeping through from the back of the house they had left via the front.

The first door on the left was the bedroom; if they were mating anywhere, Julia and her paramour, it would surely be here. But no. The door stood ajar; she peered in. The bedspread was uncreased.

Then, a misshapen cry. So near, so loud, her heart missed its rhythm.

She ducked out of the bedroom, to see a figure lurch from one of the rooms further along the landing. It took her a moment to recognize the fretful man who had arrived with Julia – and only then by his clothes. The rest was changed; horribly changed. A wasting disease had seized him in the minutes since she'd seen him on the step, shrivelling his flesh on the bone.

Seeing Kirsty, he threw himself towards her, seeking what fragile protection she could offer. He had got no more than a pace from the door however,

92

when a form spilled into sight behind him. It too seemed diseased, its body bandaged from head to foot – the bindings stained by issues of blood and pus. There was nothing in its speed, however, or the ferocity of its subsequent attack, that suggested sickness. Quite the reverse. It reached for the fleeing man and took hold of him by the neck. Kirsty let out a cry, as the captor drew its prey back into its embrace.

The victim made what little complaint his dislocated face was capable of. Then the antagonist tightened its embrace. The body trembled and twitched; its legs buckled. Blood spurted from eyes and nose and mouth. Spots of it filled the air like hot hail, breaking against her brow. The sensation snapped her from her inertia. This was no time to wait and watch. She *ran*.

The monster made no pursuit. She reached the top of the stairs without being overtaken. But as her foot descended, it addressed her.

Its voice was . . . familiar.

'There you are,' it said.

It spoke with melting tones, as if it knew her. She stopped.

'Kirsty,' it said. 'Wait a while.'

Her head told her to run. Her gut defied the wisdom however. It wanted to remember whose voice this was, speaking from the binding. She could still make good her escape, she reasoned; she had an eight-yard start. She looked round at the figure. The body in its arms had curled up, foetally, legs against chest. The beast dropped it.

'You killed him . . .' she said.

The thing nodded. It had no apologies to make, apparently, to either victim or witness.

'We'll mourn him later,' it told her, and took a step towards her.

'Where's Julia?' Kirsty demanded.

'Don't you fret. All's well . . .' the voice said. She was so close to remembering who it was.

As she puzzled it took another step, one hand upon the wall, as if its balance was still uncertain.

'I saw you . . .' it went on, 'and I think you saw me. At the window . . .' Her mystification increased. Had this thing been in the house that long? If so, surely Rory must –

And then she knew the voice.

'Yes. You do remember. I can *see* you remember . . .'

It was *Rory*'s voice or rather, a close approximation of it. More guttural; more self-regarding, but the resemblance was uncanny enough to keep her rooted to the spot while the beast shambled within snatching distance of her.

At the last she recanted her fascination, and turned to flee, but the cause was already lost. She heard its step a pace behind her, then felt its fingers at her neck. A cry came to her lips, but it was barely mounted before the thing had its corrugated palm across her face, cancelling both the shout and the breath it came upon.

It plucked her up, and took her back the way she'd come. In vain she struggled against its hold; the small wounds her fingers made upon its body – tearing at the bandages and digging into the rawness beneath – left it entirely unmoved it seemed. For a horrid moment her heels snagged the corpse on the floor. Then she was being hauled into the room from which the living and the dead had emerged. It smelt of soured milk and fresh meat. When she was flung down the boards beneath her were wet and warm.

Her belly wanted to turn inside out. She didn't fight the instinct, but retched up all that her stomach held. In the confusion of present discomfort and anticipated terror she was not certain of what happened next. Did she glimpse somebody else (Julia) on the landing as the door was slammed; or was it shadow? One way or another it was too late for appeals. She was alone with the nightmare.

Wiping the bile from her mouth she got to her feet. Daylight pierced the newspaper at the window here and there, dappling the room like sunlight through branches. And through this pastoral, the thing came sniffing her.

'Come to Daddy,' it said.

In her twenty-six years she had never heard an easier invitation to refuse.

'Don't touch me,' she told it.

It cocked its head a little, as if charmed by this show of propriety. Then it closed in on her, all pus and laughter, and – God help her – *desire*.

She backed a few desperate inches into the corner, until there was nowhere else for her to go.

'Don't you remember me?' it said.

She shook her head.

'Frank,' came the reply. 'This is brother Frank . . .'

She had met Frank only once, at Alexandra Road. He'd come visiting one afternoon, just before the

95

wedding; more she couldn't recall. Except that she'd hated him on sight.

'Leave me alone,' she said as it reached for her. There was a vile finesse in the way his stained fingers touched her breast.

'*Don't!*' she shrieked. 'Or so help me –'

'What?' said Rory's voice. 'What will you do?'

Nothing, was the answer of course. She was helpless, as only she had ever been in dreams; those dreams of pursuit and assault that her psyche had always staged on a ghetto street in some eternal night. Never – not even in her most witless fantasies – had she anticipated that the arena be a room she had walked past a dozen times, in a house where she had been happy, while outside the day went on as ever, grey on grey.

In a futile gesture of disgust, she pushed the investigating hand away.

'Don't be cruel,' the thing said, and his fingers found her skin again, as unshooable as October wasps. 'What's to be frightened of?'

'Outside . . .' she began, thinking of the horror on the landing.

'A man has to eat,' Frank replied. 'Surely you can forgive me that?'

Why did she even feel his touch? she wondered. Why didn't her nerves share her disgust and die beneath his caress?

'This isn't happening,' she told herself aloud, but the beast only laughed.

'I used to tell myself that,' he said. 'Day in, day out. Used to try and dream the agonies away. But

96

you can't. Take it from me. You can't. They have to be endured.'

She knew he was telling the truth; the kind of unsavoury truth that only monsters were at liberty to tell. He had no need to flatter or cajole; he had no philosophy to debate, or sermon to deliver. His awful nakedness was a kind of sophistication. Past the lies of faith, and into purer realms.

She knew too that she would *not* endure. That when her pleadings faltered, and Frank claimed her for whatever vileness he had in mind, she would loose such a scream that she would shatter.

Her very sanity was at stake here; she had no choice but to fight back, and quickly.

Before Frank had a chance to press his suit any harder, her hands went up to his face, fingers gouging at his eye-holes and mouth. The flesh beneath the bandage had the consistency of jelly; it came away in globs, and with it, a wet heat.

The beast shouted out, his grip on her relaxing. Seizing the moment, she threw herself out from under him, the momentum carrying her against the wall with enough force to badly wind her.

Again, Frank roared. She didn't waste time enjoying her discomfort but slid along the wall – not trusting her legs sufficiently to move into open territory – towards the door. As she advanced, her feet sent an unlidded jar of preserved ginger rolling across the room, spilling syrup and fruit alike.

Frank turned towards her, the bandaging about his face hanging in scarlet loops where she'd torn it away. In several places the bone was exposed. Even now, he ran his hands over the wounds, roars of horror coming as he sought to measure the degree of his maiming. Had she blinded him? She wasn't sure. Even if she had it was only a matter of time before he located her in this small room, and when he did his rage would know no bounds. She had to reach the door before he reoriented himself.

Faint hope! She hadn't a moment to take a step before he dropped his hands from his face and scanned the room. He saw her, no doubt of that. A beat later, he was bearing down upon her with renewed violence.

At her feet lay a litter of domestic items. The heaviest item amongst them was a plain box. She reached down and picked it up. As she stood upright, he was upon her. She loosed a cry of defiance and swung the box-bearing fist at his head. It connected heavily; bone splintered. The beast tottered backwards, and she launched herself towards the door, but before she reached it the shadow swamped her once more, and she was flung backwards across the room. Frank came in a raging pursuit.

This time he had no intention beyond the murderous. His lashes were intended to kill; that they did not was testament less to her speed than to the imprecision of his fury. Nevertheless, one out of every three blows caught her. Gashes opened in her face and upper chest; it was all she could do to prevent herself from fainting.

As she sank beneath his assault, again she remembered the weapon she'd found. The box was still in her hand. She raised it to deliver another blow, but as Frank's eyes came to rest on the box his assault abruptly ceased.

There was a panting respite, in which Kirsty had a chance to wonder if death might not be easier than further flight. Then Frank raised his arm towards her, unfurled his fist, and said: 'Give it to me . . .'

He wanted his keepsake, it seemed. But she had no intention of relinquishing her only weapon.

'No . . .' she said.

He made the demand a second time, and there was a distinct anxiety in his tone. It seemed the box was too precious for him to risk taking by force.

'One last time,' he said to her. 'Then I'll kill you. Give me the box.'

She weighed the chances; what had she left to lose?

'Say please,' she said.

He regarded her quizzically, a soft growl in his throat. Then, polite as a calculating child, said: 'Please.'

The word was her cue. She threw the box at the window with all the strength her trembling arm possessed. It sailed past Frank's head, shattering the glass, and disappeared from sight.

'*No!*' he shrieked, and was at the window in a heartbeat. '*No! No! No!*'

She raced to the door, her legs threatening to fail her with every step. Then she was out on to the landing. The stairs almost defeated her, but she clung to the banister like a geriatric, and made it to the hallway without falling.

Above, there was further din. He was calling after her again. But this time she would not be caught. She fled along the hallway to the front door, and flung it open.

The day had brightened since she'd first entered the house – a defiant burst of sunlight before evening fell. Squinting against the glare she started down the pathway. There was glass underfoot, and, amongst the shards, her weapon. She picked it up, a souvenir of her defiance, and ran. As she reached the street proper, words began to come – a hopeless babble, fragments of things seen and felt. But Lodovico Street was deserted, so she began to run, and kept running until she had put a good distance between her and the bandaged beast.

Eventually, wandering on some street she didn't recognize, somebody asked her if she needed help. The little kindness defeated her, for the effort of making some coherent reply to the enquiry was too much, and her exhausted mind lost its hold on the light.

TEN

She woke in a blizzard; or such was her first impression. Above her, a perfect whiteness; snow on snow. She was tucked up in snow; pillowed in snow. The blankness was sickening. It seemed to fill up her throat and eyes.

She raised her hands in front of her face; they smelt of an unfamiliar soap, whose perfume was harsh. Now she began to focus; the walls, the pristine sheets, the medication beside the bed. A hospital.

She called out for help. Hours or minutes later, she wasn't sure which, it came, in the form of a nurse who simply said: 'You're awake,' and went to fetch her superiors.

She told them nothing when they came. She had decided in the time between the nurse's disappearance and reappearance with the doctors that this was not a story she was ready to tell. Tomorrow (maybe) she might find the words to convince them of what she'd seen. But today? If she tried to explain they would stroke her brow and tell her to hush her nonsense; condescend to her and try to persuade her she was hallucinating. If she pressed the point, they'd probably sedate her, which would make matters worse. What she needed was time to think.

All of this she'd worked out before they arrived,

so that when they asked her what had happened she had her lies ready. It was all a fog, she told them; she could barely remember her own name. It will come back in time, they reassured her, and she replied meekly that she supposed it would. Sleep now, they said, and she told them she'd be happy to do just that, and yawned. They withdrew then.

'Oh yes ...' said one of them as he was about to go. '... I forgot ...' He brought Frank's box from his pocket. 'You were holding on to this,' he said, 'when you were found. We had the Devil's own job getting it out of your hand. Does it mean anything to you?'

She said it didn't.

'The police have looked at it. There was blood on it, you see. Maybe yours. Maybe not.'

He approached the bed.

'Do you want it?' he asked her. Then added: 'It has been cleaned.'

'Yes,' she replied. 'Yes, please.'

'It may jog your memory,' he told her, and put it down on the bedside table.

2

'What are we going to do?' Julia demanded for the hundredth time. The man in the corner said nothing; nor was there any interpretable sign on his ruin of a face. 'What did you want with her anyway?' she asked him. 'You've spoiled everything.'

102

'Spoiled?' said the monster. 'You don't know the meaning of *spoiled* . . .'

She swallowed her anger. His brooding unnerved her.

'We have to leave, Frank,' she said, softening her tone.

He threw a look across at her; white-hot ice.

'They'll come looking,' she said. 'She'll tell them everything.'

'Maybe . . .'

'Don't you *care*?' she demanded.

The bandaged lump shrugged. 'Yes,' he said. 'Of course. But we can't leave, sweetheart.' *Sweetheart*. The word mocked them both; a breath of sentiment in a room that had known only pain. 'I can't face the world like this.' He gestured to his face. 'Can I?' he said, staring up at her. 'Look at me.' She looked. '*Can I?*'

'No.'

'No.' He went back to perusing the floor. 'I need a skin, Julia.'

'A skin?'

'Then, maybe . . . maybe we can go dancing together. Isn't that what you want?'

He spoke of both dancing and death with equal nonchalance, as though one carried as little significance as the other. It calmed her, hearing him talk that way.

'How?' she said at last. Meaning, how can a skin be stolen; but also: how will our sanity survive?

'There are ways,' said the flayed face, and blew her a kiss.

Had it not been for the white walls she might never have picked up the box. Had there been a picture to look at — a vase of sunflowers, or a view of pyramids — anything to break the monotony of the room, she would have been content to stare at it, and think. But the blankness was too much; it gave her no handhold on sanity. So she reached across to the table beside the bed and picked up the box.

It was heavier than she remembered. She had to sit up in bed to examine it. There was little enough to see. No lid that she could find. No keyhole. No hinges. If she turned it over once she turned it half a hundred times, finding no clue to how it might be opened. It was not solid, she was certain of that. So logic demanded that there be a way into it. But where?

She tapped it, shook it, pulled and pressed it, all without result. It was not until she rolled over in bed and examined it in the full glare of the lamp that she discovered some clues as to how the box was constructed. There were infinitesimal cracks in the side of the box, where one piece of the puzzle abutted the next. They would have been invisible, but that a residue of blood remained in them, tracing the complex relation of the parts.

Systematically, she began to feel her way over the sides, testing her hypothesis by pushing and pulling once more. The cracks offered her a general geography of the toy; without them she might have wandered the six sides forever. But the options were significantly reduced by the clues she'd found; there were only so many ways the box could be made to come apart.

After a time, her patience was rewarded. A click, and suddenly one of the compartments was sliding out from beside its lacquered neighbours. Within, there was beauty. Polished surfaces which scintillated like the finest mother-of-pearl, coloured shadows seeming to move in the gloss.

And there was music too. A simple tune emerged from the box, played on a mechanism which she could not yet see. Enchanted, she delved further. Though one piece had been removed, the rest did not come readily. Each segment presented a fresh challenge to fingers and mind, the victories rewarded with a further filigree added to the tune.

She was coaxing the fourth section out by an elaborate series of turns and counter turns, when she heard the bell. She stopped working, and looked up.

Something was wrong. Either her weary eyes were playing tricks or the blizzard-white walls had moved subtly out of true. She put down the box, and slipped out of bed to go to the window. The bell still rang; a solemn tolling. She drew back the curtain a few inches. It was night, and windy. Leaves migrated across the hospital lawn; moths congregated in the lamplight. Unlikely as it seemed, the sound of the bell wasn't coming from outside. It was behind her. She let the curtain drop and turned back into the room.

As she did so, the bulb in the bedside light guttered like a living flame. Instinctively, she reached for the pieces of the box; they and these strange events were intertwined somehow. As her hand found the fragments, the light blew out.

She was not left in darkness, however, nor was she alone. There was a soft phosphorescence at the end of the bed; and in its folds, a figure. The condition of its flesh beggared her imagination – the hooks, the scars. Yet its voice, when it spoke, was not that of a creature in pain.

'It's called the Lemarchand Configuration,' it said, pointing at the box. She looked down; the pieces were no longer in her hand, but floating inches above her palm. Miraculously, the box was reassembling itself without visible aid, the pieces sliding back together as the whole construction turned over and over. As it did so she caught fresh glimpses of the polished interior, and seemed to see ghosts' faces – twisted as if by grief or bad glass – howling back at her. Then all but one of the segments was sealed up, and the visitor was claiming her attention afresh.

'The box is a means to break the surface of the real,' it said. 'A kind of invocation by which we Cenobites can be notified – '

'Who?' she said.

'You did it in ignorance,' the visitor said. 'Am I right?'

'Yes.'

'It's happened before,' came the reply. 'But there's no help for it. No way to seal the Schism, until we take what's ours . . .'

'This is a mistake – '

'Don't try to fight. It's quite beyond your control. You have to accompany me.'

She shook her head. She'd had enough of bullying nightmares to last her a lifetime.

'I won't go with you,' she said. 'Damn you, I won't – '

As she spoke, the door opened. A nurse she didn't recognize – a member of the night shift presumably – was standing there.

'Did you call out?' she asked.

Kirsty looked at the Cenobite, then back at the nurse. They stood no more than a yard apart.

'She doesn't see me,' it told her. 'Nor hear me. I belong to you, Kirsty. And you to me.'

'No,' she said.

'Are you sure?' said the nurse. 'I thought I heard – '

Kirsty shook her head. It was lunacy; all lunacy.

'You should be in bed,' the nurse chided. 'You'll catch your death.'

The Cenobite tittered.

'I'll be back in five minutes,' said the nurse. 'Please go back to sleep.'

And she was gone again.

'We'd better go,' it said. 'Leave them to their patchwork, eh? Such depressing places.'

'You can't do this,' she insisted.

It moved towards her nevertheless. A row of tiny bells, depending from the scraggy flesh of its neck, tinkled as it approached. The stink it gave off made her want to heave.

'Wait,' she said.

'No tears, please. It's a waste of good suffering.'

'The box,' she said, in desperation. 'Don't you want to know where I got the box?'

'Not particularly.'

'Frank Cotton,' she said. 'Does the name mean anything to you? Frank Cotton.'

The Cenobite smiled.

'Oh yes. We know Frank.'

'He solved the box too, am I right?'

'He wanted pleasure, until we gave it to him. Then he squirmed.'

'If I took you to him . . .'

'He's alive then?'

'Very much alive.'

'And you're proposing what? That I take him back instead of you?'

'*Yes. Yes. Why not! Yes.*'

The Cenobite moved away from her. The room sighed.

'I'm tempted,' it said. Then: 'But perhaps you're cheating me. Perhaps this is a lie, to buy you time.'

'I know where he *is*, for God's sake,' she said. 'He did this to me!' She presented her slashed arms for its perusal.

'If you're lying –' it said, ' – if you're trying to squirm your way out of this –'

'I'm not.'

'Deliver him alive to us then . . .'

She wanted to weep with relief.

'. . . make him confess himself. And maybe we won't tear your soul apart.'

ELEVEN

Rory stood in the hallway and stared at Julia, *his* Julia, the woman he had once sworn to have and to hold till death did them part. It had not seemed such a difficult promise to keep at the time. He had idolized her for as long as he could remember, dreaming of her by night and spending the days composing love-poems of wild ineptitude to her. But things had changed, and he had learned, as he watched them change, that the greatest torments were often the subtlest. There had been times of late when he would have preferred a death by wild horses to the itch of suspicion that had so degraded his joy.

Now, as he looked at her standing at the bottom of the stairs, it was impossible for him to even remember how good things had once been. All was doubt and dirt.

One thing he was glad of: she looked troubled. Maybe that meant there was a confession in the air, indiscretions that she would pour out and that he would forgive her for in a welter of tears and understanding.

'You look sad,' he said.

She hesitated, then said: 'It's difficult, Rory.'

'What is?'

She seemed to want to give up before she began.

'What is?' he pressed.

'I've so much to tell you.'

Her hand, he saw, was grasping the banister so tightly the knuckles burned white. 'I'm listening,' he said. He could love her again, if she'd just be honest with him. 'Tell me,' he said.

'I think maybe . . . maybe it would be easier if I *showed* you . . .' she told him, and so saying, led him upstairs.

2

The wind that harried the streets was not warm, to judge by the way the pedestrians drew their collars up and their faces down. But Kirsty didn't feel the chill. Was it her invisible companion who kept the cold from her – cloaking her with that fire the Ancients had conjured to burn sinners in? Either that, or she was too frightened to feel anything.

But then that wasn't how she felt; she *wasn't* frightened. The feeling in her gut was far more ambiguous. She had opened a door – the same door Rory's brother had opened – and now she was walking with demons. And at the end of her travels, she would have her revenge. She would find the thing that had torn her and tormented her, and make him feel the powerlessness which she had suffered. She would watch him squirm. More: she would enjoy it. Pain had made a sadist of her.

As she made her way along Lodovico Street she

looked round for a sign of the Cenobite, but he was nowhere to be seen. Undaunted, she approached the house. She had no plan in mind: there were too many variables to be juggled. For one, would Julia be there – and if so, how involved in all this was she? Impossible to believe that she could be an innocent bystander, but perhaps she had acted out of terror of Frank; the next few minutes might furnish the answers. She rang the bell, and waited.

The door was answered by Julia. In her hand, a length of white lace.

'Kirsty,' she said, apparently unfazed by her appearance. 'It's late . . .'

'Where's Rory?' were Kirsty's first words. They hadn't been quite what she'd intended, but they came out unbidden.

'He's here,' Julia replied calmly, as if seeking to soothe a manic child. 'Is there something wrong?'

'I'd like to see him,' Kirsty answered.

'Rory?'

'Yes . . .'

She stepped over the threshold without waiting for an invitation. Julia made no objection, but closed the door behind her.

Only now did Kirsty feel the chill. She stood in the hallway and shivered.

'You look terrible . . .' said Julia plainly.

'I was here this afternoon,' she blurted, 'I saw what happened, Julia. I *saw*.'

'What was there to see?' came the reply; her poise was unassailed.

'You know.'

'Truly I don't.'

111

'I want to speak to Rory . . .'

'Of course,' came the reply. 'But take care with him, will you? He's not feeling very well.'

She led Kirsty through to the dining room. Rory was sitting at the table; there was a glass of spirits at his hands, a bottle beside it. Laid across an adjacent chair was Julia's wedding dress. The sight of it prompted recognition of the lace swathe in her hand: it was the bride's veil.

Rory looked much the worse for wear. There was dried blood on his face, and at his hairline. The smile he offered was warm, but fatigued.

'What happened . . . ?' she asked him.

'It's all right now, Kirsty,' he said. His voice barely aspired to a whisper. 'Julia told me everything . . . and it's all right.'

'No,' she said, knowing that he couldn't possibly have the whole story.

'You came here this afternoon.'

'That's right.'

'That was unfortunate.'

'You . . . you asked me . . .' She glanced at Julia, who was standing at the door, then back at Rory. 'I did what I thought you wanted.'

'Yes. I know. I know. I'm only sorry you were dragged into this terrible business – '

'You know what your brother's done?' she said. 'You know what he summoned?'

'I know enough,' Rory replied. 'The point is, it's over now.'

'What do you mean?'

'Whatever he did to you, I'll make amends – '

'What do you mean, *over*?'

112

'He's dead, Kirsty.'

('. . . *deliver him alive, and maybe we won't tear your soul apart.*')

'Dead?'

'We destroyed him, Julia and I. It wasn't too difficult. He thought he could trust me, you see; thought that blood was thicker than water. Well it isn't. I wouldn't suffer a man like that to live . . .'

She felt something twitch in her belly. Had the Cenobites got their hooks in her already, snagging the carpet of her bowels?

'You've been so kind, Kirsty. Risking so much, coming back here . . .'

(There was something at her shoulder. '*Give me your soul,*' it said.)

'. . . I'll go to the authorities, when I feel a little stronger. Try and find a way to make them understand . . .'

'You killed him?' she said.

'Yes.'

'I don't believe it . . .' she muttered.

'Take her upstairs,' Rory said to Julia, 'show her.'

'Do you want to see?' Julia enquired.

Kirsty nodded, and followed.

It was warmer on the landing than below, and the air greasy and grey, like filthy dish-water. The door to Frank's room was ajar. The thing that lay on the bare boards, in a tangle of torn bandaging, still steamed. His neck was clearly broken, his head askew on his shoulders. He was devoid of skin from head to foot.

Kirsty looked away, nauseated.

'Satisfied?' Julia asked.

Kirsty didn't reply, but left the room and stepped on to the landing. At her shoulder, the air was restless.

('*You lost*,' something said, close by her.

'I know,' she murmured.)

The bell had begun to ring, tolling for her, surely; and a turmoil of wings nearby, a carnival of carrion-birds. She hurried down the stairs, praying that she wouldn't be overtaken before she reached the door. If they tore her heart out, let Rory be spared the sight. Let him remember her strong; with laughter on her lips, not pleas.

Behind her, Julia said: 'Where are you going?' When there was no reply forthcoming she went on talking. 'Don't say anything to anybody, Kirsty,' she insisted. 'We can deal with this, Rory and me –'

Her voice had stirred Rory from his drink. He appeared in the hallway. The wounds Frank had inflicted looked more severe than Kirsty had first thought. His face was bruised in a dozen places, and the skin at his neck ploughed up. As she came abreast of him, he reached out and took her arm.

'Julia's right,' he said. 'Leave it to us to report, will you?'

There were so many things she wanted to tell him at that moment, but time left room for none. The bell was getting louder in her head. Someone had looped their entrails around her neck, and was pulling the knot tight.

'It's too late . . .' she murmured to Rory, and pressed his hand away.

'What do you mean?' he said to her, as she covered

114

the yards to the door. 'Don't go, Kirsty. Not yet. Tell me what you mean.'

She couldn't help but offer him a backwards glance, hoping that he would find in her face all the regrets she felt.

'It's all right,' he said sweetly, still hoping to heal her. 'Really it is.' He opened his arms. '*Come to Daddy*,' he said.

The phrase didn't sound right out of Rory's mouth. Some boys never grew to be Daddies, however many children they sired.

Kirsty put out a hand to the wall to steady herself.

It wasn't Rory who was speaking to her. It was Frank. Somehow, it was Frank —

She held on to the thought through the mounting din of bells, so loud now that her skull seemed ready to crack open. Rory was still smiling at her, arms extended. He was talking too, but she could no longer hear what he said. The tender flesh of his face shaped the words, but the bells drowned them out. She was thankful for the fact; it made it easier to defy the evidence of her eyes.

'I know who you are . . .' she said suddenly, not certain of whether her words were audible or not, but unquenchably sure that they were true. Rory's corpse was upstairs; left to lie in Frank's shunned bandaging. The usurped skin was now wed to his brother's body, the marriage sealed with the letting of blood. Yes! That was it.

The coils around her throat were tightening; it could only be moments before they dragged her off. In desperation, she started back along the hallway towards the thing in Rory's face.

'It's you – ' she said.

The face smiled at her, undismayed.

She reached out, and snatched at him. Startled, he took a step backwards to avoid her touch; moving with graceful sloth, but somehow still managing to avoid her touch. The bells were intolerable; they were pulping her thoughts, tolling her brain tissue to dust. At the rim of her sanity, she reached again for him, and this time he did not quite avoid her. Her nails raked the flesh of his cheek, and the skin, so recently grafted, slid away like silk. The blood-battered meat beneath came into horrid view.

Behind her, Julia screamed.

And suddenly the bells weren't in Kirsty's head any longer. They were in the house; in the world.

The hallway lights burned dazzlingly bright, and then – their filaments overloading – went out. There was a short period of total darkness, during which time she heard a whimpering which may or may not have come from her own lips. Then it was as if fireworks were spluttering into life in the walls and floor. The hallway danced. One moment an abattoir (the walls running scarlet); the next, a boudoir (powder blue, canary yellow); the moment following that, a ghost-train tunnel – all speed and sudden fire.

By one flaring light she saw Frank moving towards her, Rory's discarded face hanging from his jaw. She avoided his outstretched arm and ducked through into the front room. The hold on her throat had relaxed, she realized, the Cenobites had apparently seen the error of their ways. Soon they would intervene, surely, and bring an end to this farce of mistaken identities. She would not wait to see Frank

116

claimed as she'd thought of doing; she'd had enough. Instead she'd flee the house by the back door, and leave them to it.

Her optimism was short-lived. The fireworks in the hall threw some light ahead of her into the dining room; enough to see that it was already bewitched. There was something moving over the floor, like ash before wind, and chairs cavorting in the air. Innocent she might be, but the forces loose here were indifferent to such trivialities; she sensed that to take another step would invite atrocities.

Her hesitation put her back within Frank's reach, but as he snatched at her the fireworks in the hallway faltered, and she slipped away from him under cover of darkness. The respite was all too brief. New lights were already blooming in the hall – and he was after her afresh, blocking her route to the front door.

Why didn't they claim him, for God's sake? Hadn't she brought them here as she'd promised, and unmasked him?

Frank opened his jacket. In his belt was a bloodied knife – doubtless the flaying edge. He pulled it out, and pointed it at Kirsty.

'From now on,' he said, as he stalked her, 'I'm Rory . . .' She had no choice but to back away from him, the door (escape; sanity) receding with every step. 'Understand me? I'm Rory now. And nobody's ever going to know any better.'

Her heel hit the bottom of the stair, and suddenly there were other hands on her, reaching through the banisters and seizing fistfuls of her hair. She twisted her head round and looked up. It was Julia of course, face slack, all passion consumed. She wrenched

Kirsty's head back, exposing her throat as Frank's knife gleamed towards it.

At the last moment Kirsty reached up above her head and snatched hold of Julia's arm, wrenching her from her perch on the third or fourth stair. Losing both her balance and her grip on her victim, Julia let out a shout and fell, her body coming between Kirsty and Frank's thrust. The blade was too close to be averted; it entered Julia's side to the hilt. She moaned, then she reeled away down the hall, the knife buried in her.

Frank scarcely seemed to notice. His eyes were on Kirsty once again, and they shone with horrendous appetite. She had nowhere to go but *up*. The fireworks still exploding, the bells still ringing, she started to mount the stairs.

Her tormentor was not coming in immediate pursuit, she saw. Julia's appeals for help had diverted him to where she lay, halfway between stairs and front door. He drew the knife from her side. She cried out in pain, and, as if to assist her, he went down on his haunches besides her body. She raised her arm to him, looking for tenderness. In response, he cupped his hand beneath her head, and drew her up towards him. As their faces came within inches of each other, Julia seemed to realize that Frank's intentions were far from honourable. She opened her mouth to scream, but he sealed her lips with his and began to feed. She kicked and scratched the air. All in vain.

Tearing her eyes from the sight of this depravity, Kirsty crawled up to the head of the stairs.

The second floor offered no real hiding place, of

course, nor was there any escape route, except to leap from one of the windows. But having seen the cold comfort Frank had just offered his mistress, jumping was clearly the preferable option. The fall might break every bone in her body, but it would at least deprive the monster of further sustenance.

The fireworks were fizzling out, it seemed; the landing was in smoky darkness. She stumbled along it rather than walked, her fingertips tracing the wall.

Downstairs, she heard Frank on the move again. He was finished with Julia.

Now he spoke as he began up the stairs, the same incestuous invitation: '*Come to Daddy*.'

It occurred to her that the Cenobites were probably viewing this chase with no little amusement, and would not act until there was only one player left: Frank. She was forfeit to their pleasure.

'Bastards . . .' she breathed, and hoped they heard.

She had almost reached the end of the landing. Ahead lay the junk room. Did it have a window sizeable enough for her to climb through? If so, she would jump, and curse them as she fell – curse them all, God and the Devil and whatever lay between, curse them and hope for nothing as she dropped but that the concrete be quick with her.

Frank was calling her again, and almost at the top of the stairs. She turned the key in the lock, opened the junk room door, and slipped through.

Yes, there was a window. It was uncurtained, and moonlight fell through it in shafts of indecent beauty, illuminating a chaos of furniture and boxes. She made her way through the confusion to the window. It was wedged open an inch or two, to air the room.

She put her fingers under the frame, and tried to heave it up far enough for her to climb out, but the sash in the window had rotted, and her arms were not the equal of the task.

She quickly hunted for a makeshift lever, a part of her mind coolly calculating the number of steps it would take her pursuer to cover the length of the landing. Less than twenty, she concluded, as she pulled a sheet off one of the tea chests, only to find a dead man staring up at her from the chest, eyes wild. He was broken in a dozen places, arms smashed and bent back upon themselves, legs tucked up to his chin. As she went to cry out, she heard Frank at the door.

'Where are you?' he enquired.

She clamped her hand over her face to stop the cry of revulsion from coming. As she did so, the door-handle turned. She ducked out of sight behind a felled armchair, swallowing her scream.

The door opened. She heard Frank's breath, slightly laboured; heard the hollow pad of his feet on the boards. Then the sound of the door being pulled to again. It clicked. Silence.

She waited for a count of thirteen, then peeped out of hiding, half expecting him to still be in the room with her, waiting for her to break cover. But no, he'd gone.

Swallowing the breath her cry had been mounting upon had brought an unwelcome side-effect: hiccups. The first of them, so unexpected she had no time to subdue it, sounded gun-crack loud. But there were no returning steps from the landing. Frank, it seemed, was already out of earshot. As she returned to the window, skirting the tea-chest coffin, a second hiccup startled her. She silently reprimanded her belly, but in vain. A third and fourth came unbidden while she wrestled once more to lift the window. That too was a fruitless effort; it had no intention of compliance.

Briefly, she contemplated breaking the glass and yelling for help, but rapidly discarded the idea. Frank would be eating out her eyes before the neighbours had even shaken off sleep. Instead she retraced her steps to the door, and opened it a creaking fraction. There was no sign of Frank, so far as her eyes were able to interpret the shadows. Cautiously, she opened the door a little wider, and stepped on to the landing once again.

The gloom was like a living thing; it smothered her with murky kisses. She advanced three paces without incident, then a fourth. On the fifth (her lucky number) her body took a turn for the suicidal. She hiccupped, her hand too tardy to reach her mouth before the din was out.

This time it did not go unheard.

'There you are,' said a shadow, and Frank slipped from the bedroom to block her path. He was vaster for his meal – he seemed as wide as the landing – and he stank of meat.

With nothing to lose, she screamed blue murder as he came at her. He was unshamed by her terror. With inches between her flesh and his knife she threw herself sideways and found that the fifth step had brought her abreast of Frank's room. She stumbled through the door. He was after her in a flash, crowing his delight.

There was a window in this room, she knew; she'd

broken it herself, mere hours before. But the darkness was so profound she might have been blindfolded; not even a glimmer of moonlight to feed her sight. Frank was equally lost, it seemed. He called after her in this pitch; the whine of his knife accompanying his call as he slit the air. Back and forth, back and forth. Stepping away from the sound, her foot caught in the tangle of bandaging on the floor. Next moment she was toppling. It wasn't the boards she fell heavily upon, however, but the greasy bulk of Rory's corpse. It won a howl of horror from her.

'There you are,' said Frank. The knife slices were suddenly closer, inches from her head. But she was deaf to them. She had her arms about the body beneath her, and approaching death was nothing beside the pain she felt now, touching him.

'Rory,' she moaned, content that his name be on her lips when the cut came.

'That's right,' said Frank, '. . . Rory.'

Somehow the theft of Rory's name was as unforgivable as stealing his skin; or so her grief told her. A skin was nothing. Pigs had skins; snakes had skins. They were knitted of dead cells, shed and grown and shed again. But a name? That was a spell, which summoned memories. She would not let Frank usurp it.

'Rory's dead,' she said. The words stung her, and with the sting, the ghost of a thought.

'Hush, baby . . .' he told her.

Suppose the Cenobites were waiting for Frank to name himself? Hadn't the visitor in the hospital said something about Frank *confessing*?

'You're not Rory . . .' she said.

'*We* know that,' came the reply, 'but nobody else does . . .'

'Who are you then?'

'Poor baby. Losing your mind, are you? Good thing too . . .'

'Who, though?'

'. . . it's safer that way.'

'*Who*?'

'Hush, baby,' he said. He was stooping to her in the darkness, his face within inches of hers. 'Everything's going to be as right as rain . . .'

'Yes?'

'Yes. Frank's here, baby.'

'Frank?'

'That's right. I'm *Frank*.'

So saying, he delivered the killing blow, but she heard it coming in the darkness, and dodged its benediction. A second later the bell began again, and the bare bulb in the middle of the room flickered into life. By it she saw Frank beside his brother, the knife buried in the dead man's buttock. As he worked it out of the wound he set his eye on her afresh.

Another chime, and he was up, and would have been at her . . . but for the voice.

It said his name, lightly, as if calling a child out to play.

'Frank.'

His face dropped for the second time that night. A look of puzzlement flitted across it, and on its heels, horror.

Slowly, he turned his head round to look at the speaker. It was the Cenobite, its hooks sparkling.

Behind it, Kirsty saw three other figures, their ana-
tomies catalogues of disfigurement.

Frank threw a glance back at Kirsty.

'You did this,' he said.

She nodded.

'Get out of here,' said one of the newcomers. 'This
isn't your business now.'

'Whore!' Frank screeched at her. 'Bitch! *Cheating,
fucking bitch!*'

The hail of rage followed her across the room to
the door. As her palm closed around the door-handle
she heard him coming after her, and turned to find
that he was standing less than a foot from her, the
knife a hair's breadth from her body. But there he
was fixed, unable to advance another millimetre.

They had their hooks in him, the flesh of his arms
and legs, and curled through the meat of his face.
Attached to the hooks, chains, which they held taut.
There was a soft sound, as his resistance drew the
barbs through his muscle. His mouth was dragged
wide, his neck and chest ploughed open.

The knife dropped from his fingers. He expelled a
last, incoherent curse at her, his body shuddering
now as he lost his battle with their claim upon him.
Inch by inch he was drawn back towards the middle
of the room.

'*Go,*' said the voice of the Cenobite. She could see
them no longer; they were already lost behind the
blood-flecked air. Accepting their invitation, she
opened the door while behind her Frank began to
scream.

As she stepped on to the landing plaster dust cas-
caded from the ceiling; the house was growling from

124

basement to eaves. She had to go quickly, she knew, before whatever demons were loose here shook the place apart.

But, though time was short, she could not prevent herself from snatching one look at Frank to be certain that he would come after her no longer.

He was *in extremis*; hooked through in a dozen or more places, fresh wounds gouged in him even as she watched. Spreadeagled beneath the solitary bulb, body hauled to the limits of its endurance and beyond, he gave vent to shrieks that would have won pity from her, had she not learned better.

Suddenly, his cries stopped. There was a pause. And then, in one last act of defiance, he cranked up his heavy head and stared at her, meeting her gaze with eyes from which all bafflement and all malice had fled. They glittered as they rested on her; pearls in offal.

In response, the chains were drawn an inch tighter, but the Cenobites gained no further cry from him. Instead he put his tongue out at Kirsty and flicked it back and forth across his teeth in a gesture of unrepentant lewdness.

Then he came unsewn.

His limbs separated from his torso, and his head from his shoulders, in a welter of bone shards and heat. She threw the door closed, as something thudded against it from the other side. His head, she guessed.

Then she was staggering downstairs, with wolves howling in the walls, and the bells in turmoil, and everywhere – thickening the air like smoke – the ghosts of wounded birds, sewn wing-tip to wing-tip, and lost to flight.

She reached the bottom of the stairs, and began along the hallway to the front door, but as she came within spitting distance of freedom she heard some-one call her name.

It was Julia. There was blood on the hall floor, marking a trail from the spot where Frank had abandoned her through into the dining room.

'Kirsty . . .' she called again. It was a pitiable sound, and despite the wing-choked air, she could not help but go in pursuit of it, stepping through into the dining room.

The furniture was smouldering charcoal; the ash that she'd glimpsed was a foul-smelling carpet. And there, in the middle of this domestic wasteland, sat a bride. By some extraordinary act of will, Julia had managed to put her wedding dress on, and secure her veil upon her head. Now she sat in the dirt, the dress besmirched. But she looked radiant nevertheless; more beautiful, indeed, for the fact of the ruin that surrounded her.

'Help me,' she said, and only now did Kirsty realize that the voice she heard was not coming from beneath the lush veil, but from the bride's lap.

And now the copious folds of the dress were parting, and there was Julia's head – set on a pillow of scarletted silk, and framed with a fall of auburn hair. Bereft of lungs, how could it speak? It spoke nevertheless –

'Kirsty . . .' it said, it begged – and sighed, and rolled back and forth in the bride's lap as if it hoped to unlodge its reason.

Kirsty might have aided it — might have snatched the head up and dashed out its brains — but that the bride's veil had started to twitch, and was rising now, as if plucked at by invisible fingers. Beneath it, a light flickered and grew brighter, and brighter yet; and with the light, a voice.

'*I am the Engineer,*' it sighed. No more than that. Then the fluted folds rose higher, and the head beneath gained the brilliance of a minor sun.

She did not wait for the blaze to blind her. Instead she backed out into the hallway — the birds almost solid now, the wolves insane — and flung herself at the front door even as the hallway ceiling began to give way.

The night came to meet her — a clean darkness. She breathed it in greedy gulps as she departed the house at a run. It was her second such departure. God help her sanity then should there ever be a third.

At the corner of Lodovico Street, she looked back. The house had not capitulated to the forces unleashed within. It stood now as quiet as a grave. No; *quieter*.

As she turned away somebody collided with her. She yelped with surprise, but the huddled pedestrian was already hurrying away into the anxious murk that preceded morning. As the figure hovered on the outskirts of solidity, it glanced back, and its head flared in the gloom, a cone of white fire. It was the Engineer. She had no time to look away; it was gone again in one instant, leaving its glamour in her eye.

Only then did she realize the purpose of the collision. Lemarchand's box had been passed back to her, and sat in her hand.

Its surface had been immaculately resealed, and

polished to a high gloss. Though she did not examine it, she was certain there would be no clue to its solution left. The next discoverer would voyage its faces without a chart. And until such time, was she elected its keeper? Apparently so.

She turned it over in her hand. For the frailest of moments she seemed to see ghosts in the lacquer. Julia's face, and that of Frank. She turned it over again, looking to see if Rory was held here: but no. Wherever he was, it wasn't here. There were other puzzles, perhaps, that if solved gave access to the place where he lodged. A crossword maybe, whose solution would lift the latch of the paradise garden; or a jigsaw in the completion of which lay access to Wonderland.

She would wait and watch, as she had always watched and waited, hoping that such a puzzle would one day come to her. But if it failed to show itself she would not grieve too deeply, for fear that the mending of broken hearts be a puzzle neither wit nor time had the skill to solve.

Clive Barker

IMAJICA

Clive Barker's new novel, *Imajica*, is published by HarperCollins in October 1991. An extract from the opening chapters is printed in the following pages.

'Magic is the first and last religion of the world.
It has the power to make us whole, to open
our eyes to the Dominions, and return us to ourselves.
We're born divided, and long for union.
We're joined to everything that was, is and will be.
From one end of the Imajica to the other.'

Amid a seamless tapestry of erotic passion, thwarted ambition and mythic horror, *Imajica* picks out the brightly coloured threads of three memorable characters: John Furie Zacharias, known as Gentle, a master forger whose own life is a series of lies; Judith Odell, a beautiful woman desired by three powerful men, but belonging to none of them; and Pie'oh'pah, a mysterious assassin who deals in love as well as death. United in a desperate search for the heart of a universal mystery, all three discover the truth that lies in a place as mysterious as the face of God, and as secret as the human soul. They discover the Imajica.

The Imajica: five Dominions, four reconciled, and one, the Earth, cut off from them, her inhabitants living in ignorance on the edge of a sea of possibilities, an ocean of mystery and magic. Only a few know of the Imajica, and many of them are frightened. For a time is coming, a time of great risk, a time of great promise – a shining mystical moment in which Earth can be reunited with the other four Dominions. A time of Reconciliation.

As Judith, Gentle and Pie race to capture that moment, other forces are gathering to keep the Earth forever bound in the darkness that surrounds her. Their quest will carry them on an epic journey through all five Dominions to the very border of the greatest mystery of all: the First Dominion, on the other side of which lies the Holy City of the Unbeheld, where their highest hopes, or their deepest fears, will be realized.

Imajica – a book of revelations – is Clive Barker's outstanding achievement to date. Spellspinner, master fabulist, he takes us on a voyage to worlds beyond our knowledge, but within our grasp. Long after you have turned the final page, you will be yearning for *Imajica*'s wonders, believing they are just a breath away.

At dusk the clouds over Manhattan, which had threatened snow all day, cleared, and revealed a pristine sky, its colour so ambiguous it might have fuelled a philosophical debate as to the nature of blue. Laden as she was with her day's purchases, Jude chose to walk back to Marlin's apartment at Park Avenue and 80th. Her arms ached, but it gave her time to turn over in her head the encounter which had marked the day, and decide whether she wanted to share it with Marlin or not. Unfortunately, he had a lawyer's mind. At best, cool and analytical; at worst, reductionist. She knew herself well enough to know that if he challenged her account in the latter mode she'd almost certainly lose her temper with him, and then the atmosphere between them, which had been (with the exception of his overtures) so easy and undemanding, would be spoiled. It was better to work out what she believed about the events of the previous two hours before she shared it with Marlin. Then he could dissect it at will.

Already, after going over the encounter a few times, it was becoming, like the blue overhead, ambiguous. But she held on hard to the facts of the matter. She'd been in the menswear department of Bloomingdale's, looking for a sweater for Marlin. It was crowded, and there was nothing on display that she thought appropriate. She'd bent down to pick up the purchases at her feet, and as she rose again she'd caught sight of a face she knew, looking straight at her through the moving mesh of people. How long had she seen the face for? A second; two at most? Long enough for her heart to jump, and her face to flush; long enough for her mouth to open and shape the word *Gentle*. Then the traffic between them had thickened, and he'd disappeared. She'd fixed the place where he'd been, stooped to pick up her baggage, and gone after him, not doubting that it was he.

The crowd slowed her progress, but she soon caught sight of him again, heading towards the door. This time she yelled his name, not giving a damn if she looked a fool, and dived after him. She was impressive in full flight, and the crowd yielded, so that by the time she reached the door he was only yards the other side. Third Avenue was as thronged as the store, but there he was, heading across the street. The lights changed as she got to the kerb. She went after him anyway, daring the traffic. As she yelled again he was buffeted by a shopper about some business as urgent as hers, and he turned as he was struck, giving her a second glimpse of him. She might have laughed out loud at the absurdity of her error had it not disturbed her so. Either she was losing her mind, or she'd followed the wrong man. Either way, this black man, his ringleted hair gleaming on his shoulders, was not Gentle. Momentarily undecided as to whether to go on looking or to give up the chase there and then, her eyes lingered on the stranger's face, and for a heartbeat, or less, his features blurred, and in their flux, caught as if by the sun off a wing in the stratosphere, she saw Gentle, his hair swept back from his high forehead, his grey eyes all yearning, his mouth, which she'd not known she missed till now, ready to break into a smile. It never came. The wing dipped, the stranger turned, Gentle was gone. She stood in the throng for several seconds while he disappeared downtown. Then, gathering herself together, she turned her back on the mystery, and started home.

It didn't leave her thoughts, of course. She was a woman who trusted her senses, and to discover them so deceptive distressed her. But more vexing still was why it should be that particular face, of all those in her memory's catalogue, she'd chosen to configure from that of a perfect stranger. Klein's Bastard Boy was out of her life, and she out of his. It was six years since she'd crossed the bridge from where they'd stood, and the river that flowed between was a torrent. Her marriage to Estabrook had come and gone along that river, and a good deal of pain with it. Gentle was still on the other shore, part of her history; irretrievable. So why had she conjured him now?

As she came within a block of Marlin's building she remembered something she'd utterly put out of her head for that six-year span. It had been a glimpse of Gentle, not so unlike the one she'd just had, that had propelled her into her near-suicidal affair with him. She'd met him at one of Klein's parties – a casual encounter – and had given him very little conscious thought subsequently. Then, three nights later, she'd been visited by an erotic dream that regularly haunted her. The scenario was always the same. She was lying naked on bare boards in an empty room, not bound but somehow bounded, and a man whose face she could never see, his mouth so sweet it was like eating candy to kiss him, made violent love to her. Only this time the fire that burned in the grate close by showed her the face of her dream-lover, and it had been Gentle's face. The shock, after so many years of never knowing who the man was, woke her, but with such a sense of loss at this interrupted coitus she couldn't sleep again for mourning it. The next day she'd discovered his whereabouts from Klein, who'd warned her in no uncertain manner that John Zacharias was bad news for tender hearts. She'd ignored the warning, and gone to see him that afternoon, in the studio off the Edgware Road. They scarcely left it for the next two weeks, their passion putting her dreams to shame.

Only later, when she was in love with him and it was too late for common sense to qualify her feelings, did she learn more about him. He trailed a reputation for womanizing that, even if it was ninety per cent invention, as she assumed, was still prodigious. If she mentioned his name in any circle, however jaded it was by gossip, there was always somebody who had some titbit about him. He even went by a variety of names. Some referred to him as the Furie; some as Zach or Zacho, or Mr Zee; others called him Gentle, which was the name she knew him by, of course; still others, John the Divine. Enough names for half a dozen lifetimes. She wasn't so blindly devoted to him that she didn't accept there was truth in these rumours. Nor did he do much to temper them. He liked the air of legend that hung about his head. He claimed, for instance, not to know how old he was. Like herself, he had a very slippery grasp on the past. And he frankly admitted to being obsessed with her sex – some of the talk she'd heard was of cradle-snatching; some of death-bed fucks – he played no favourites.

So, here was her Gentle: a man known to the doormen of every exclusive club and hotel in the city, who, after ten years of high-living, had survived the ravages of every excess; who was still lucid, still handsome, still alive. And this same man, this Gentle, told her he was in love with her, and put the words together so perfectly she disregarded all she'd heard but those he spoke.

She might have gone on listening forever, but for her rage, which was the legend *she* trailed. A volatile thing, apt to ferment in her without her even being aware of it. That had been the case with Gentle. After half a year of their affair, she'd begun to wonder, wallowing in his affection, how a man whose history had been one infidelity after another had mended his ways; which thought led to the possibility that perhaps he hadn't. In fact she had no reason to suspect him. His devotion bordered on the obsessive in some moods, as though he saw in her a woman she didn't even know herself, an ancient soul-mate. She was, she began to think, unlike any other woman he'd ever met; the love that had changed his life. When they were so intimately joined, how would she not know if he were cheating on her? She'd have surely sensed the other woman. Tasted her on his tongue, or smelt her on his skin. And if not there, then in the subtleties of their exchanges. But she'd underestimated him. When, by the sheerest fluke, she'd discovered he had not one other woman on the side but two, it drove her to near insanity. She began by destroying the contents of the studio, slashing all his canvases, painted or not, then tracking the felon himself, and mounting an assault that literally brought him to his knees, in fear for his balls.

The rage burned a week, after which she fell totally silent for three days; a silence broken by a grief like nothing she'd ever experienced before. Had it not been for her chance meeting with Estabrook – who saw through her tumbling, distracted manner to the woman she was – she might well have taken her own life. Thus the tale of Judith and Gentle: one death short of tragedy, and a marriage short of farce.

She found Marlin already home, uncharacteristically agitated.

'Where have you been?' he wanted to know. 'It's six thirty-nine.'

She instantly knew this was no time to be telling him what her trip to Bloomingdale's had cost her in peace of mind. Instead she lied. 'I couldn't get a cab. I had to walk.'

'If that happens again just call me. I'll have you picked up by one of our limos. I don't want you wandering the streets. It's not safe. Anyhow, we're late. We'll have to eat after the performance.'

'What performance?'

'The show in the Village Troy was yabbering about last night, remember? The Neo-Nativity? He said it was the best thing since Bethlehem.'

'It's sold out.'

'I have my connections,' he gleamed.

'We're going tonight?'

'Not if you don't move your ass.'

'Marlin, sometimes you're sublime,' she said, dumping her purchases and racing to change.

'What about the rest of the time?' he hollered after her. 'Sexy? Irresistible? Beddable?'

If indeed he'd secured the tickets as a way of bribing her between the sheets, then he suffered for his lust. He concealed his boredom through the first act, but by the intermission he was itching to be away to claim his prize.

'Do we really need to stay for the rest?' he asked her as they sipped coffee in the tiny foyer. 'I mean, it's not like there's any mystery about it. The kid gets born, the kid grows up, the kid gets crucified.'

'I'm enjoying it.'

'But it doesn't make any sense,' he complained, in deadly earnest. The show's eclecticism offended his rationalism deeply. 'Why were the angels playing jazz?'

'Who knows what angels do?'

He shook his head. 'I don't know whether it's a comedy, or a satire or what the hell it is,' he said. 'Do you know what it is?'

'I think it's very funny.'

'So you'd like to stay?'

'I'd like to stay.'

The second half was even more of a grab-bag than the first, the suspicion growing in Jude as she watched that the parody and pastiche was a smoke-screen put up to cover the creators' embarrassment at their own sincerity. In the end, with Charlie Parker angels wailing on the stable roof, and Santa crooning at the manger, the piece collapsed into high camp. But even that was oddly moving. The child was born. Light had come into the world again, even if it was to the accompaniment of tap-dancing elves.

When they exited, there was sleet in the wind.

'Cold, cold, cold,' Marlin said. 'I'd better take a leak.'

He went back inside to join the queue for the toilets, leaving Jude at the door watching the blobs of wet snow pass through the lamp-light. The theatre was not large, and the bulk of the audience were out in a couple of minutes, umbrellas raised, heads dropped, darting off into the Village to look for their cars, or a place where they could put some drink in their systems, and play critics. The light above the front door was switched off, and a cleaner emerged from the theatre with a black plastic bag of rubbish and a broom, and began to brush the foyer, ignoring Jude – who was the last visible occupant – until he reached her, when he gave her a glance of such venom she decided to put up her umbrella and stand on the darkened step. Marlin was taking his time emptying his bladder. She only hoped he wasn't titivating himself, slicking his hair and freshening his breath in the hope of talking her into bed.

The first she knew of the assault was a motion glimpsed from the corner of her eye: a blurred form approaching her at speed through the thickening sleet. Alarmed, she turned towards her attacker. She had time to recognize the face on Third Avenue, then the man was upon her.

She opened her mouth to yell, turning to retreat into the theatre as she did so. The cleaner had gone. So had her shout, caught in her throat by the stranger's hands. They were expert. They hurt brutally, stopping every breath from being drawn. She panicked; flailed; toppled. He took her weight, controlling her motion. In desperation she threw the umbrella into the foyer, hoping there was somebody out of sight in the box-office who'd be alerted to her jeopardy. Then she was wrenched out of shadow into heavier shadow still, and realized it was almost too late already. She was becoming light-headed; her leaden limbs no longer hers. In the murk her assassin's face was once more a blur, with two dark holes bored in it. She fell towards them, wishing she had the energy to turn her gaze away from this blankness, but as he moved closer to her a little light caught his cheek and she saw, or thought she saw, tears there, spilling from those dark eyes. Then the light went, not just from his cheek but from the whole world. And as everything slipped away she could only hold on to the thought that somehow her murderer knew who she was—

'*Judith?*'

Somebody was holding her. Somebody was shouting to her. Not the assassin, but Marlin. She sagged in his arms, catching dizzied sight of the assailant running across the pavement, with another man in pursuit. Her eyes swung back towards Marlin, who was asking her if she was all right, then back towards the street as brakes shrieked, and the failed assassin was struck squarely by a speeding car, which reeled round, wheels locked and sliding over the sleet-greased street, throwing the man's body off the bonnet and over a parked car. The pursuer threw himself aside as the vehicle mounted the pavement, slamming into a lamppost.

Jude put her arm out for some support other than Marlin, her fingers finding the wall. Ignoring his advice that she stay still, stay still, she started to stumble towards the place where her assassin had fallen. The driver was being helped from his smashed vehicle, unleashing a stream of obscenities as he emerged. Others were appearing on the scene to lend help in forming a crowd, but Jude ignored their stares and headed across the street, Marlin at her side. She was determined to reach the body before anybody else. She wanted to see it before it was touched; wanted to meet its open eyes and fix its dead expression; know it, for memory's sake.

She found his blood first, spattered in the grey slush underfoot, and then, a little way beyond, the assassin himself, reduced to a lumpen form in the gutter. As she came within a few yards of it, however, a shudder passed down its spine, and it rolled over, showing its face to the sleet. Then, impossible though this seemed given the blow it had been struck, the form started to haul itself to its feet. She saw how bloodied it was, but she saw also that it was still essentially whole. It's not human, she thought, as it stood upright; whatever it is, it's not human. Marlin groaned with revulsion behind her, and a woman on the pavement screamed. The man's gaze went to the screamer, wavered, then returned to Jude.

It wasn't an assassin any longer. Nor was it Gentle. If it had a self, perhaps this was its face: split by wounds and doubt; pitiful; lost. She saw its mouth open and close as if it was attempting to address her. Then Marlin made a move to pursue it, and it ran. How, after such an accident, its limbs managed any speed at all was a miracle, but it was off at a pace that Marlin couldn't hope to match. He made a show of pursuit, but gave up at the first intersection, returning to Jude breathless.

'Drugs,' he said, clearly angered to have missed his chance at heroism. 'Fucker's on drugs. He's not feeling any pain. Wait till he comes down, he'll drop dead. Fucker! How did he know you?'

'Did he?' she said, her whole body trembling now, as relief at her escape and terror at how close she'd come to losing her life both stung tears from her.

'He called you Judith,' Marlin said.

In her mind's eye she saw the assassin's mouth open and close, and on them read the syllables of her name.

'Drugs,' Marlin was saying again, and she didn't waste words arguing, though she was certain he was wrong. The only drug in the assassin's system had been purpose, and that would not lay him low, tonight or any other.

* * *

Eleven days after he had taken Estabrook to the encampment in Streatham, Chant realized he would soon be having a visitor. He lived alone, and anonymously, in a one-room flat on a soon-to-be-condemned estate close to the Elephant and Castle, an address he had given to nobody, not even his employer. Not that his pursuers would be distracted from finding him by such petty secrecy. Unlike *homo sapiens*, the species his long-dead master Sartori had been wont to call *the blossom on the simian tree*, Chant's kind could not hide themselves from oblivion's agents by closing a door and drawing the blinds. They were like beacons to those that preyed on them.

Men had it so much easier. The creatures that had made meat of them in earlier ages were zoo specimens now, brooding behind bars for the entertainment of the victorious ape. They had no grasp, those apes, of how close they lay to a state where the devouring beasts of Earth's infancy would be little more than fleas. That state was called the In Ovo, and on the other side of it lay four worlds, the so-called Reconciled Dominions. They teemed with wonders: individuals blessed with attributes that would have made them, in this, the Fifth Dominion, fit for sainthood, or burning, or both; cults possessed of secrets that would overturn in a moment the dogmas of faith and physics alike; beauty that might blind the sun, or set the moon dreaming of fertility. All this, separated from earth – the unreconciled Fifth – by the abyss of the In Ovo.

It was not, of course, an impossible journey to make. But the power to do so, which was usually – and contemptuously – referred to as magic, had been waning in the Fifth since Chant had first arrived. He'd seen the walls of reason built against it, brick by brick. He'd seen its practitioners hounded and mocked; seen its theories decay into decadence and parody; seen its purpose steadily forgotten. The Fifth was choking in its own certainties, and though he took no pleasure in the thought of losing his life, he would not mourn his removal from this hard and unpoetic Dominion.

He went to his window, and looked down the five storeys into the courtyard. It was empty. He had a few minutes yet, to compose his missive to Estabrook. Returning to his table, he began it again, for the ninth or tenth time. There was so much he wanted to communicate, but he knew that Estabrook was utterly ignorant of the involvement his family, whose name he'd abandoned, had with the fate of the Dominions. It was too late now to educate him. A warning would have to suffice. But how to word it so that it didn't sound like the rambling of a wild man? He set to again, putting the facts as plainly as he could, though doubted that these words would save Estabrook's life. If the powers that prowled this world tonight wanted him dispatched, nothing short of intervention from the Unbeheld Himself, Hapexamendios, the all-powerful occupant of the First Dominion, would save him.

With the note finished, Chant pocketed it, and headed out into the darkness. Not a moment too soon. In the frosty quiet he heard the sound of an engine too suave to belong to a resident, and peered over the parapet to see the men getting out of the car below. He didn't doubt that these were his visitors. The only vehicles he'd seen here so polished were hearses. He cursed himself. Fatigue had made him slothful, and now he'd let his enemies get dangerously close. He ducked down the back stairs – glad, for once, that there were so few lights working along the landings – as his visitors strode towards the front. From the flats he passed, the sound of lives: Christmas pops on the radio, argument, a baby laughing, which became tears, as though it sensed that there was danger near. He knew none of his neighbours, except as furtive faces glimpsed at windows, and now – though it was too late to change that – he regretted it.

He reached ground level unharmed, and discounting the thought of trying to retrieve his car from the courtyard he headed off towards the street most heavily trafficked at this time of night, which was Kennington Park Road. If he was lucky he'd find a cab there, though at this time of night they weren't frequent. Fares were harder to pick up in this area than in Covent Garden or Oxford Street, and more likely to prove unruly. He allowed himself one backward glance towards the estate, then turned his heels to the task of flight.

Though classically it was the light of day which showed a painter the deepest flaws in his handiwork, Gentle worked best at night; the instincts of a lover brought to a simpler art. In the week or so since he'd returned to his studio it had once again become a place of work: the air pungent with the smell of paint and turpentine, the burned-down butts of cigarettes left on every available shelf and plate. Though he'd spoken with Klein daily there was no sign of a commission yet, so he had spent the time re-educating himself. As Klein had so cruelly observed, he was a technician without a vision, and that made these days of meandering difficult. Until he had a style to forge, he felt listless, like some latter-day Adam, born with the power to impersonate but bereft of subjects. So he set himself an exercise. He would paint a canvas in four radically different styles: a cubist North, an impressionist South, an East after Van Gogh, a West after Dali. As his subject he took Caravaggio's *Supper at Emmaus*. The challenge drove him to a healthy distraction, and he was still occupied with it at three thirty in the morning, when the telephone rang. The line was watery, and the voice at the other end pained and raw, but it was unmistakably Judith.

'Is that you, Gentle?'

'It's me.' He was glad the line was so bad. The sound of her voice had shaken him, and he didn't want her to know. 'Where you calling from?'

'New York. I'm just visiting for a few days.'

'It's good to hear from you.'

'I'm not sure why I'm calling. It's just that today's been strange and I thought maybe, oh—' She stopped. Laughed at herself, perhaps a little drunkenly. 'I don't know what I thought.' She went on: 'It's stupid. I'm sorry.'

'When are you coming back?'

'I don't know that either.'

'Maybe we could get together?'

'I don't think so, Gentle.'

'Just to talk.'

'This line's getting worse. I'm sorry I woke you.'

'You didn't—'

'Keep warm, huh?'

'Judith—'

'Sorry, Gentle.'

The line went dead. But the water she'd spoken through gurgled on, like the noise in a sea-shell. Not the ocean at all, of course; just illusion. He put the receiver down, and – knowing he'd never sleep now – squeezed out some fresh bright worms of paint to work with, and set to.

It was the whistle from the gloom behind him that alerted Chant to the fact that his escape had not gone unnoticed. It was not a whistle that could have come from human lips, but a chilling scalpel shriek he had heard only once before in the Fifth Dominion, when, some two hundred years past, his then possessor, the Maestro Sartori, had conjured from the In Ovo a familiar which had made such a whistle. It had brought bloody tears to its summoner's eyes, obliging Sartori to relinquish it post-haste. Later Chant and the Maestro had spoken of the event, and Chant had identified the creature. It was a creature known in the Reconciled Dominions as a voider, one of a brutal species that haunted the wastes North of the Lenten Way. Voiders came in many shapes, being made, some said, from collective desire, which fact seemed to move Sartori profoundly.

'I must summon one again,' he'd said, 'and speak with it.' To which Chant had replied that if they were to attempt such a summoning they had to be ready next time, for voiders were lethal, and could not be tamed except by Maestros of inordinate power. The proposed conjuring had never taken place. Sartori had disappeared a short time later. In all the intervening years Chant had wondered if he had attempted a second summoning alone, and been the voiders' victim. Perhaps the creature coming after Chant now had been responsible. Though Sartori had disappeared two hundred years ago, the lives of voiders, like those of so many species from the other Dominions, were longer than the longest human span.

Chant glanced over his shoulder. The whistler was in sight. It looked perfectly human, dressed in a grey, well-cut suit and black tie, its collar turned up against the cold, its hands thrust into its pockets. It didn't run, but almost idled as it came, the whistle confounding Chant's thoughts, and making him stumble. As he turned away, the second of his pursuers appeared on the pavement in front of him, drawing its hand from its pocket. A gun? No. A knife. No. Something tiny crawling in the voiders' palm, like a flea. Chant had no sooner focused upon it than it leapt towards his face. Repulsed, he raised his arm to keep it from his eyes or mouth, and the flea landed upon his hand. He slapped at it with his other hand, but it was beneath his thumbnail before he could get to it. He raised his arm to see its motion in the flesh of his thumb, and clamped his other hand around the base of the digit in the hope of stopping its further advance, gasping as though doused with ice-water. The pain was out of all proportion to the mite's size, but he held both thumb and sobs hard, determined not to lose all dignity in front of his executioners. Then he staggered off the pavement into the street, throwing a glance down towards the brighter lights at the junction. What safety they offered was debatable, but if worst came to worst he would throw himself beneath a car, and deny the voider the entertainment of his slow demise. He began to run again, still clutching his hand. This time he didn't glance back. He didn't need to. The sound of the whistling

Imajica 17

faded, and the purr of the car replaced it. He threw every ounce of his energy into the run, reaching the bright street to find it deserted by traffic. He turned north, racing past the underground station towards the Elephant and Castle. Now he did glance behind, to see the car following steadily. It had three occupants. The voiders, and another, sitting in the back seat. Sobbing with breathlessness he ran on, and – Lord love it! – a taxi appeared around the next corner, its yellow light announcing its availability. Concealing his pain as best he could, knowing the driver might pass on by if he thought the hailer was wounded, he stepped out into the street, and raised his hand to wave the driver down. This meant unclasping one hand from the other, and the mite took instant advantage, working its way up into his wrist. But the vehicle slowed.

'Where to, mate?'

He astonished himself with the reply, giving not Estabrook's address, but that of another place entirely.

'Clerkenwell,' he said, 'Gamut Street.'

'Don't know it,' the cabbie replied, and for one heart-stopping moment Chant thought he was going to drive on.

'I'll direct you,' he said.

'Get in, then.'

Chant did so, slamming the cab door with no little satisfaction, and barely managing to reach the seat before the cab picked up speed.

Why had he named Gamut Street? There was nothing there that would heal him. Nothing could. The flea – or whatever variation in that species it was that crawled in him – had reached his elbow, and his arm below that pain was now completely numb, the skin of his hand wrinkled and flaky. But the house in Gamut Street had been a place of miracles once. Men and women of great authority had walked in it, and perhaps left some ghost of themselves to calm him *in extremis*. No creature, Sartori had taught, passed through this Dominion unrecorded, even to the least – to the child that perished a heartbeat after it opened its eyes, the child that died in the womb, drowned in its mother's waters – even that unnamed thing had its record and its consequence. So how much more might the once-mighty of Gamut Street have left, by way of echoes?

His heart was palpitating, and his body full of jitters. Fearing he'd soon lose control of his functions, he pulled the letter to Estabrook from his pocket, and leaned forward to slide the half-window between himself and the driver aside.

'When you've dropped me in Clerkenwell I'd like you to deliver a letter for me. Would you be so kind?'

'Sorry, mate,' the driver said, 'I'm going home after this. I've a wife waiting for me.'

Chant dug in his inside pocket and pulled out his wallet, then passed it through the window, letting it drop on the seat beside the driver.

'What's this?'

'All the money I've got. This letter has to be delivered.'

'All the money you've got, eh?'

The driver picked up the wallet and flicked it open, his gaze going between its contents and the road.

'There's a lot of dosh in here.'

'Have it. It's no good to me.'

'Are you sick?'

'And tired,' Chant said. 'Take it, why don't you? Enjoy it.'

'There's a Daimler been following us. Somebody you know?'

There was no purpose served by lying to the man. 'Yes,' Chant said, 'I don't suppose you could put some distance between them and us?'

The man pocketed the wallet, and jabbed his foot down on the accelerator. The cab leapt forward like a race horse from a gate, its jockey's laugh rising above the guttural din of the engine. Whether it was the cash he was now heavy with or the challenge of out-running a Daimler that motivated him, he put his cab through its paces, proving it more mobile than its bulk would have suggested. In under a minute they'd made two sharp lefts and a squealing right, and were roaring down a back street so narrow the least miscalculation would have taken off handles, hubs and mirrors. The mazing didn't stop there. They made another turn, and another, bringing them in a short time to Southwark Bridge. Somewhere along the way, they'd lost the Daimler. Chant might have applauded had he possessed two workable hands, but the flea's message of corruption was spreading with agonizing speed. While he still had five fingers under his command he went back to the window and dropped Estabrook's letter through, murmuring the address with a tongue that felt disfigured in his mouth.

'What's wrong with you?' the cabbie said. 'It's not fucking contagious is it, 'cause if it is—'

' . . . not . . .' Chant said.

'You look fucking awful,' the cabbie said, glancing in the mirror. 'Sure you don't want a hospital?'

'No. Gamut Street. I want Gamut Street.'

'You'll have to direct me from here.'

The streets had all changed. Trees gone; rows demolished; austerity in place of elegance, function in place of beauty; the new for old, however poor the exchange rate. It was a decade and more since he'd come here last. Had Gamut Street fallen, and a steel phallus risen in its place?

'Where are we?' he asked the driver.

'Clerkenwell. That's where you wanted, isn't it?'

'I mean the precise place.'

The driver looked for a sign. 'Flaxen Street. Does it ring a bell?'

Chant peered out of the window. 'Yes! Yes! Go down to the end, and turn right.'

'Used to live around here, did you?'

'A long time ago.'

'It's seen better days.' He turned right. 'Now where?'

'First on the left.'

'Here it is,' the man said. 'Gamut Street. What number was it?'

'Twenty-eight.'

The cab drew up at the curb. Chant fumbled for the handle, opened the door, and all but fell out on to the pavement. Staggering, he put his weight against the door to close it, and for the first time he and the driver came face to face. Whatever the flea was doing to his system it must have been horribly apparent, to judge by the look of repugnance on the man's face.

'You *will* deliver the letter?' Chant said.

'You can trust me, mate.'

'When you've done it, you should go home,' Chant said. 'Tell your wife you love her. Give a prayer of thanks.'

'What for?'

'That you're human,' Chant said.

The cabbie didn't question this little lunacy.

'Whatever you say, mate,' he replied. 'I'll give the missus one and give thanks at the same time, how's that? Now don't do anything I wouldn't do, eh?'

This advice given, he drove off, leaving his passenger to the silence of the street.

With failing eyes, Chant scanned the gloom. The houses, built in the middle of Sartori's century, looked to be mostly deserted; primed for demolition perhaps. But then Chant knew that sacred places — and Gamut Street was sacred in its way — survived on occasion because they went unseen, even in plain sight. Burnished by magic, they deflected the threatening eye and found unwitting allies in men and women who, all unknowing, knew holiness; became sanctuaries for a secret few.

He climbed the three steps to the door, and pushed at it, but it was securely locked, so he went to the nearest window. There was a filthy shroud of cobweb across it, but no curtain beyond. He pressed his face to the glass. Though his eyes were weakening by the moment, his gaze was still more acute than that of the blossoming ape. The room he was looking into was stripped of all furniture and decoration; if anybody had occupied this house since Sartori's time — and it surely hadn't stood empty for two hundred years – they had gone, taking every trace of their presence. He raised his good arm and struck the glass with his elbow, a single jab which shattered the window. Then, careless of the damage he did himself, he hoisted his bulk onto the sill, beat out the rest of the pieces of glass with his hand, and dropped down into the room on the other side.

The layout of the house was still clear in his mind. In dreams he'd drifted through these rooms, and heard the Maestro's voice summoning him up the stairs, up! up!, to the room at the top where Sartori had worked his work. It was there Chant wanted to go now, but there were new signs of atrophy in his body with every heartbeat. The hand first invaded by the flea was withered, its nails dropped from their place, its bone showing at the knuckles and wrist. Beneath his jacket he knew his torso to the hip was similarly unmade; he felt pieces of his flesh falling inside his shirt as he moved. He would not be moving for much longer. His legs were increasingly unwilling to bear him up, and his senses were close to flickering out. Like a man whose children were leaving him he begged as he climbed the stairs:

'Stay with me. Just a little longer. *Please* . . .'

His cajoling got him as far as the first landing, but then his legs all but gave out, and thereafter he had to climb using his one good arm to haul him onwards.

He was halfway up the final flight when he heard the voiders whistle in the street outside, its piercing din unmistakable. They had found him quicker than he'd anticipated, sniffing him out through the darkened streets. The fear that he'd be denied sight of the sanctum at the top of the stairs spurred him on, his body doing its ragged best to accommodate his ambition.

From below, he heard the door being forced open. Then the whistle again, harder than before, as his pursuers stepped into the house. He began to berate his limbs, his tongue barely able to shape the words.

'Don't let me down! Work, will you? *Work!*'

And they obliged. He scaled the last few stairs in a spastic fashion, but reached the top flight as he heard the voiders' soles at the bottom. It was dark up here, though how much of that was blindness and how much night he didn't know. It scarcely mattered. The route to the door of the sanctum was as familiar to him as the limbs he'd lost. He crawled on hand and knees across the landing, the ancient boards creaking beneath him. A sudden fear seized him: that the door would be locked, and he'd beat his weakness against it, and fail to gain access. He reached up for the handle, grasped it, tried to turn it once, failed, tried again, and this time dropped face-down over the threshold as the door swung open.

There was food for his enfeebled eyes. Shafts of moonlight spilled from the windows in the roof. Though he'd dimly thought it was sentiment that had driven him back here, he saw now it was not. In returning here he came full circle, back to the room which had been his first glimpse of the Fifth Dominion. This was his cradle, and his tutoring room. Here he'd smelt the air of England for the first time, the crisp October air; here he'd fed first, drunk first; first had cause for laughter, and later, for tears. Unlike the lower rooms, whose emptiness was a sign of desertion, this space had always been sparely furnished, and sometimes completely empty. He'd danced here on the same legs that now lay dead beneath him, while Sartori had told him how he planned to take this wretched Dominion, and build in its midst a city that would shame Babylon; danced for sheer exuberance, knowing his Maestro was a great man, and had it in his power to change the world.

Lost ambition; all lost. Before that October had become November Sartori had gone, flitted in the night, or murdered by his enemies. Gone, and left his servant stranded in a city he barely knew. How Chant had longed then to return to the ether from where he'd been summoned; to shrug off the body which Sartori had congealed around him, and be gone out of this Dominion. But the only voice capable of ordering such a release was that which had conjured him, and with Sartori gone, he was exiled on earth forever. He hadn't hated his summoner for that. Sartori had been indulgent for the weeks they'd been together. Were he to appear now, in the moonlit room, Chant would not have accused him of negligence, but made proper obeisances and been glad that his inspiration had returned.

' . . . Maestro . . .' he murmured, face to the musty boards.

'Not here,' came a voice from behind him. It was not, he knew, one of the voiders. They could whistle, but not speak. 'You were Sartori's creature, were you? I don't remember that.'

The speaker was precise, cautious and smug. Unable to turn, Chant had to wait until the man walked past his supine body to get a sight of him. He knew better than to judge by appearances. He, whose flesh was not his own, but of the Maestro's sculpting. Though the man in front of him looked human enough, he had the voiders in tow, and spoke with knowledge of things few humans had access to. His face was an overripe cheese, drooping with jowls and weary folds around the eyes, his expression that of funereal comic. The smugness in his voice was here too, in the studied way he licked upper and lower lips with his tongue before he spoke, and tapped the fingertips of each hand together as he judged the broken man at his feet. He wore an immaculately tailored three-piece suit, cut from a cloth of apricot cream. Chant would have given a good deal to break the bastard's nose so he bled on it.

'I never did meet Sartori,' he said. 'Whatever happened to him?'

The man went down on his haunches in front of Chant and suddenly snatched hold of a handful of his hair.

'I asked you what happened to your Maestro,' he said. 'I'm Dowd, by the way. You never knew *my* master, the Lord Godolphin, and I never knew yours. But they're gone, and you're scrabbling around for work. Well, you won't have to do it any longer, if you take my meaning.'

'Did you . . . did you send him to me?'

'It would help my comprehension if you could be more specific.'

'Estabrook.'

'Oh yes. Him.'

'You did. Why?'

'Wheels within wheels, my dove,' Dowd said. 'I'd tell you the whole bitter story, but you don't have the time to listen and I don't have the patience to explain. I knew of a man who needed an assassin. I knew of another man who dealt in them. Let's leave it at that.'

'But how did you know about me?'

'You're not discreet,' Dowd replied. 'You get drunk on the Queen's birthday, and you gab like an Irishman at a wake. Lovey, it draws attention sooner or later.'

'Once in a while . . .'

'I know, you get melancholy. We all do, lovey, we all do. But some of us do our weeping in private, and some of us' – he let Chant's head drop – 'make fucking public spectacles of ourselves. There are *consequences*, lovey, didn't Sartori tell you that? There are always *consequences*. You've begun something with this Estabrook business, for instance, and I'll need to watch it closely, or before we know it there'll be ripples, spreading through the Imajica.'

' . . . the Imajica . . .'

'That's right. From here to the margin of the First Dominion. To the region of the Unbeheld Himself.'

Chant began to gasp, and Dowd – realizing he'd hit a nerve – leaned towards his victim.

'Do I detect a little anxiety?' he said. 'Are you afraid of going into the glory of our Lord Hapexamendios?'

Chant's voice was frail now. ' . . . yes . . .' he murmured.

'Why?' Dowd wanted to know. 'Because of your crimes?'

'Yes.'

'What *are* your crimes? Do tell me. We needn't bother with the little things. Just the really shameful stuff'll do.'

'I've had dealings with a Eurhetemec.'

'Have you indeed?' Dowd said. 'How ever did you get back to Yzorderrex to do that?'

'I didn't,' Chant replied. 'My dealings . . . were here in the Fifth.'

'Really,' said Dowd, softly. 'I didn't know there were Eurhetemecs here. You learn something new every day. But, lovey, that's no great crime. The Unbeheld's going to forgive a poxy little trespass like that. Unless . . . He stopped for a moment, turning over a new possibility. 'Unless, the Eurhetemec was a *mystif* . . .' He trailed the thought, but Chant remained silent. 'Oh, my dove,' Dowd said. 'It wasn't, was it?' Another pause. 'Oh, it *was*. It *was*.' He sounded almost enchanted. 'There's a mystif in the Fifth, and what? You're in love with it? You'd better tell me before you run out of breath, lovey. In a few minutes your eternal soul will be waiting at Hapexamendios' door.'

Chant shuddered. 'The assassin . . .' he said.

'What *about* the assassin?' came the reply. Then realizing what he'd just heard, Dowd drew a long, slow breath. 'The assassin is a mystif?' he said.

'Yes.'

'Oh, my sweet Hyo!' he exclaimed. 'A mystif!' The enchantment had vanished from his voice now. He was hard and dry. 'Do you know what they can do? The deceits they've got at their disposal? This was supposed to be an anonymous piece of shit-stirring, and look what you've done!' His voice softened again. 'Was it beautiful?' he asked. 'No, no. Don't tell me. Let me have the surprise, when I see it face to face.' He turned to the voiders. 'Pick the fucker up,' he said.

They stepped forward, and raised Chant by his

broken arms. There was no strength left in his neck, and his head lolled forward, a solid stream of bilious fluid running from his mouth and nostrils. 'How often does the Eurhetemec tribe produce a mystif?' Dowd mused, half to himself. 'Every ten years? Every fifty? They're certainly rare. And there you are, blithely hiring one of these little divinities as an assassin. Imagine! How pitiful, that it had fallen so low. I must ask it how that came about . . .' He stepped towards Chant, and at Dowd's order one of the voiders raised Chant's head by the hair. 'I need the mystif's whereabouts,' Dowd said. 'And its name.'

Chant sobbed through his bile. ' . . . please . . .' he said. ' . . . I meant . . . I . . . meant . . .'

'Yes, yes. No harm. You were just doing your duty. The Unbeheld will forgive you, I guarantee it. But the *mystif*, lovey, I need you to tell me about the mystif. Where can I find it? Just speak the words, and you won't ever have to think about it again. You'll go into the presence of the Unbeheld like a babe.'

'I will?'

'You will. Trust me. Trust me. Just give me its name, and tell me the place where I can find it.'

'Name . . . and . . . place.'

'That's right. But get to it, lovey, before it's too late!'

Chant book as deep a breath as his collapsing lungs allowed. 'It's called Pie'oh'pah,' he said.

Dowd stepped back from the dying man as if slapped. 'Pie'oh'pah? Are you sure?'

' . . . I'm sure . . .'

'Pie'oh'pah is alive? And Estabrook hired it?'

'Yes?'

Dowd threw off his imitation of a Father Confessor, and murmured a fretful question of himself. 'What does this mean?' he said.

Chant made a pained little moan, his system racked by further waves of dissolution. Realizing that time was now very short, Dowd pressed the man afresh.

'Where *is* this mystif? Quickly, now! *Quickly!*'

Chant's face was decaying, cobs of withered flesh sliding off his slickened bone. When he answered, it was with half a mouth. But answer he did, to be unburdened.

'I thank you,' Dowd said to him, when all the information had been supplied. 'I thank you.' Then, to the voiders, 'Let him go.'

They dropped Chant without ceremony. When he hit the floor his face broke, pieces spattering Dowd's shoe. He viewed the mess with disgust.

'Clean it off,' he said.

The voiders were at his feet in moments, dutifully removing the scraps of matter from Dowd's hand-made shoes.

'What does this mean?' Dowd murmured again. There was surely synchronicity in this turn of events. In a little over half a year's time the anniversary of the Reconciliation would be upon the Imajica. Two hundred years would have passed since the Maestro Sartori had attempted, and failed, to perform the greatest act of magic known to this or any other Dominion. The plans for that ceremony had been laid here, at number twenty-eight Gamut Street, and the mystif, amongst others, had been there to witness the preparations.

The ambition of those heady days had ended in

tragedy, of course. Rites intended to heal the rift in the Imajica, and reconcile the Fifth Dominion with the other four, had gone disastrously awry. Many great theurgists, shamans and theologians had been killed. Determined that such a calamity never be repeated, several of the survivors had banded together in order to cleanse the Fifth of all magical knowledge. But however much they scrubbed to erase the past, the slate could never be entirely cleansed. Traces of what had been dreamed and hoped for remained; fragments of poems to Union, written by men whose names had been systematically removed from all record. And as long as such scraps remained, the spirit of the Reconciliation would survive.

But spirit was not enough. A maestro was needed; a magician arrogant enough to believe that he could succeed where Christos and innumerable other sorcerers, most lost to history, had failed. Though these were blissless times, Dowd didn't discount the possibility of such a soul appearing. He still encountered in his daily life a few who looked past the empty gaud that distracted lesser minds and longed for a revelation that would burn the tinsel away, an Apocalypse that would show the Fifth the glories it yearned for in its sleep.

If a Maestro was going to appear, however, he would need to be swift. Another attempt at Reconciliation couldn't be planned overnight, and if the next mid-summer went unused, the Imajica would pass another two centuries divided. Time enough for the Fifth Dominion to destroy itself out of boredom or frustration, and prevent the Reconciliation from ever taking place.

Dowd perused his newly polished shoes.

'Perfect,' he said. 'Which is more than I can say for the rest of this wretched world.'

He crossed to the door. The voiders lingered by the body, however, bright enough to know that they still had some duty to perform with it. But Dowd called them away.

'We'll leave it here,' he said. 'Who knows? It may stir a few ghosts.'